ALSO BY ALEJO CARPENTIER

NOVELS

Praised Be the Lord!

The Lost Steps

The Chase

Explosion in a Cathedral

Reasons of State

The Rite of Spring

The Harp and the Shadow

STORIES

The War of Time

ESSAYS

Music in Cuba

THE KINGDOM
OF THIS WORLD

THE KINGDOM
OF THIS WORLD

<><><><><><><><><><><><><><><><><><><><><><><>

Alejo Carpentier

Translated from the Spanish by Pablo Medina

Farrar, Straus and Giroux

New York

Farrar, Straus and Giroux
18 West 18th Street, New York 10011

Printed in the United States of America
Originally published in Spanish in 1949 by E.D.I.A.P.S.A., Mexico, D.F.,
as *El reino de este mundo*
This translation originally published in the United States by
Farrar, Straus and Giroux
First edition, 2017

Library of Congress Cataloging-in-Publication Data
Names: Carpentier, Alejo, 1904–1980, author. | Medina, Pablo,
   1948– translator.
Title: The kingdom of this world / Alejo Carpentier ; translated
   from the Spanish by Pablo Medina.
Other titles: Reino de este mundo. English
Description: First paperback edition. | Farrar, Straus and Giroux :
   New York, 2017. | "Originally published in Spanish in 1949 by
   E.D.I.A.P.S.A., Mexico, D.F., as El Reino de Este Mundo"—Verso
   title page. | A translation by Harriet de Onís was published by
   Farrar, Straus and Giroux in 1989, and reissued in 2006.
Identifiers: LCCN 2017001320 | ISBN 9780374537388 (pbk.)
Subjects: LCSH: Haiti—History—Revolution, 1791–1804—Fiction.
Classification: LCC PQ7389.C263 R413 2017 | DDC 863/.64—dc23
LC record available at https://lccn.loc.gov/2017001320

Designed by Jonathan D. Lippincott

Our books may be purchased in bulk for promotional, educational,
or business use. Please contact your local bookseller or the Macmillan
Corporate and Premium Sales Department at 1-800-221-7945, extension
5442, or by e-mail at MacmillanSpecialMarkets@macmillan.com.

www.fsgbooks.com
www.twitter.com/fsgbooks • www.facebook.com/fsgbooks

9   10   8

Contents

Introduction by Edwidge Danticat *vii*
Preface *xiii*

PART ONE
1. Wax Heads   3
2. The Pruning   10
3. What the Hand Discovered   13
4. The Account   17
5. De Profundis   20
6. The Metamorphosis   24
7. In Human Dress   28
8. The Great Flight   31

PART TWO
1. The Daughter of Minos and Pasiphaë   37
2. The Great Covenant   42
3. The Call of the Conch Shells   46
4. Dagon Inside the Ark   49

CONTENTS

5. Santiago de Cuba   54

6. The Ship of Dogs   59

7. Saint Calamity   65

PART THREE

1. The Signs   73

2. Sans-Souci   76

3. The Sacrifice of the Bulls   81

4. Walled In   86

5. Chronicle of August Fifteenth   91

6. *Ultima Ratio Regum*   95

7. The Only Gate   103

PART FOUR

1. The Night of the Statues   111

2. The Royal House   119

3. The Surveyors   123

4. *Agnus Dei*   127

Afterword by Pablo Medina   *133*

Introduction

by Edwidge Danticat

In January 2004 Haiti observed the two-hundred-year an-
niversary of its independence from France in the midst
of a national revolt. In the capital, as well as other cities
throughout the country, pro- and antigovernment dem-
onstrators clashed. Members of a disbanded army declared
war on a young and inexperienced police force. Mobs of
angry young men, some called *chimè* (chimeras) by their
countrymen and others calling themselves cannibals, bat-
tled one another to assure that then Haitian president Jean-
Bertrand Aristide—worshipped by chimeras and reviled
by cannibals—either remained in office or left.

A few weeks later Aristide departed in the early hours
of a Sunday morning. By his account, he was kidnapped
from his residence in Port-au-Prince and put on a U.S. jet,
which took him to the Central African Republic, where he
was held prisoner for several weeks. By other accounts,
he went willingly, even signing a letter of resignation in
Haitian Creole. As Aristide began his life in exile, he

echoed in his statements to the international press nearly the same words that Toussaint L'Ouverture—one of the principal leaders of the first successful slave uprising in history—uttered when he was forced to board a ship headed for a prison in France: "In overthrowing me, you have cut . . . only the trunk of the tree of liberty. It will spring up again from the roots, for they are numerous and deep."

Haitians were not surprised that Aristide chose to link his exit with such a powerful reverberation of the past. After all, there has been no more evocative moment in Haiti's history than the triumphant outcome of the revolution that L'Ouverture had lived and died for. Though Haiti's transition from slavery to free state was far from seamless, many Haitians, myself included, would rather forget the schisms that followed independence, the color and class divisions that split the country into sections ruled by self-declared monarchs who governed exactly as they had been governed, with little regard for parity or autonomy.

In *The Kingdom of This World*, Alejo Carpentier allows us to consider the possibility—something which his own Cuba would later grapple with—that a revolution that some consider visionary might appear to others to have failed. Through the eyes of Ti Noël—neither king nor ruler but an ordinary man—we get an intimate view of the key players in an epic story that merges myth and lore with meticulously detailed facts and astonishing lyricism. That this book is so short seems almost miraculous, for even with leaps in time and place, one feels neither shorthanded nor cheated, because the words and sentences are as carefully mounted as the walls of the massive citadel that the ambitious King Henri Christophe commands and Ti Noël and his countrymen build. What might take a more long-winded writer an entire book, Carpentier covers in one chapter. Yet we still encounter some of the most memorable architects of the Haitian revolution, along with some fictional comrades they pick up along the way. We meet the one-armed Mackandal, who is said to have turned into an insect in order to escape his fiery execution; Bouckman—most commonly spelled Boukman—who held the stirring Vodou ceremony that helped transform Toussaint L'Ouverture from mild-mannered herbalist to heroic warrior. And of course we come to know King Christophe, a former restaurateur, who shoots himself with a silver bullet but not before forcing his countrymen to experience the "rebirth of shackles, this proliferation of miseries, which the least hopeful accepted as proof of the uselessness of any sort of revolt."

Though Ti Noël does not remain among the resigned for too long, he is certainly tested through his disheartening encounters with those who have shaped (and misshaped) his country's destiny. What we ultimately must accept is that he is neither phantom observer nor ubiquitous witness. Like Haiti itself, he cannot be easily defined. At most, one might see Ti Noël as a stand-in for Carpentier.

Born of a Russian mother and French father, Carpentier

shows with his skillful handling of this narrative that the essence of a revolution lies not only in its instantaneous burst of glory but in its arduous ripples across borders and time, its ability to shame the conquerors and fortify the oppressed, and, in some cases, to achieve the opposite. For if history is recounted by victors, it's not easy to tell here who the rightful narrators should be, unless we keep redefining with each page what it means to conquer and be conquered.

Carpentier once disclosed that during a trip to Haiti in the 1940s he found himself in daily contact with something he called the *real maravilloso*, or the "marvelous real."

"I was stepping on ground whereon thousands of people eager for freedom believed," he wrote in the preface to the 1949 edition. "I had visited the Citadelle of La Ferrière, a building without architectural precedent . . . I had breathed the atmosphere created by Henri Christophe, a monarch of remarkable endeavors . . . Every step I took, I came across the marvelous real."

The marvelous real, which we have come to know as magical realism, lives and thrives in past and present Haiti, just as it does in this novel. It is in the extraordinary and the mundane, the beautiful and the repulsive, the spoken and the unspoken. It is in the enslaved African princes who knew the paths of the clouds and the language of the forests of their homelands but could no longer recognize themselves in the so-called New World. It is in Damballah, the snake god; in Ogun, the god of war. It is in the elaborate cornmeal drawings sketched in the soil at Vodou ceremonies to seek help from these *loas* or spirits. From Haiti's fertile communal imagination sprang a fantastic sense of possibility, which certainly contributed to bondmen and -women defeating the most powerful armies of the time.

Whenever possible, Haitians cite their cosmic connection to this heroic heritage by invoking the names of one or all of the founders of our country: Toussaint L'Ouverture, Henri Christophe, and Jean-Jacques Dessalines. (The latter's fighting creed during the Haitian war of independence was *Koupe tèt, boule kay* ["Cut heads, burn houses"].)

"They can't do this to us," we say today when feeling subjugated. "We are the children of Toussaint L'Ouverture, Henri Christophe, and Jean-Jacques Dessalines."

As President Aristide's opportune evocation of L'Ouverture shows, for many of us, it is as though the Haitian revolution were fought two hundred days, rather than two centuries, ago. This book reminds us why this remains so. For is there anything more timely and timeless than a public battle to control one's destiny, a communal crusade for self-determination? The outcome, when it's finally achieved, can be nearly impossible to describe. It certainly was for one Haitian poet who was given the task of drafting Haiti's Act of Independence. To do it appropriately, Boisrond-Tonnerre declared, he would need the skin of a former master—a white man—for parchment, his skull for an inkwell, his blood for ink, and a bayonet for a pen.

Though not inscribed with the same intention, Carpentier's words have no less sting or power.

EDWIDGE DANTICAT was born in Haiti and moved to the United States when she was twelve. She is the author of several books, including *Breath, Eyes, Memory*; *Krik? Krak!*; *The Farming of Bones*; and *The Dew Breaker*.

Preface

> ... What we must understand about this matter of turning into wolves is that there is a malady the doctors call lupine mania ...
>
> —Miguel de Cervantes, *The Labors of Persiles and Sigismunda*

At the end of 1943 I was fortunate enough to visit the kingdom of Henri Christophe (the poetic ruins of Sans-Souci; the massive Citadelle of La Ferrière, impressively intact despite lightning storms and earthquakes) and to get to know the still-Norman city of the Cap, called Cap Français during colonial times, where a street of very long balconies still leads to the stone palace once occupied by Pauline Bonaparte. After feeling the all-too-real enchantment of the land of Haiti, finding signs of magic by the sides of the red roads of the central plain, and hearing the drums of Petro and Rada, I was driven to compare this recently experienced marvelous reality with the tiresome attempts to evoke the marvelous that characterized certain European literature of the last thirty years: the marvelous, pursued through the old clichés of the forest of Brocéliande, the Knights of the Round Table, Merlin the Enchanter, and the Arthurian cycle; the marvelous, poorly suggested by the stereotypes and deformities of carnival characters (will young French poets never tire of the geeks and clowns of the *fête foraine*, whom Rimbaud had already dismissed in his "Alchemy of the Word"?); the marvelous, obtained with tricks of prestidigitation by bringing together objects that have nothing in common, such as the old and deceitful story of the fortuitous encounter between the umbrella and the sewing machine on a dissection table, the generator of ermine spoons, the snails inside a raining taxi, and the head of a lion on the pelvis of a widow, all to be found in surrealist shows; or, more pertinently, the literary marvelous— the king of de Sade's *Juliette*, the supermacho of Jarry, Lewis's monk, and the hair-raising props of the English Gothic novel: ghosts, immured priests, lycanthropies, and hands nailed on the door of a castle.

By dint of wanting to elicit the marvelous at every turn, the magician becomes a bureaucrat. Invoked by means of the usual formulas that make of certain paintings a monotonous junk pile of rubbery clocks, tailor's mannequins, or vague phallic monuments, the marvelous never goes beyond an umbrella or a lobster or a sewing machine or whatever, lying on a dissection table inside a sad room in a rocky desert. Imaginative poverty, Unamuno used to say, is the consequence of learning codes by heart. And today there are codes of the fantastic, based on the principle of the donkey devoured by a fig, proposed by *Les chants de Maldoror* as the supreme inversion of reality, to which we owe all those "children threatened by nightingales," or the "horses devouring birds" of André Masson. But note that when André Masson tried to draw the jungles of the island of Martinique, with that unbelievable commingling of its plants and the obscene promiscuity of some of its fruit, the marvelous truth of the subject matter devoured the painter, leaving him at the edge of impotence before the blank paper. It had to be a painter from the Americas, the Cuban Wifredo Lam, who'd teach us the magic of tropical vegetation, the insatiable Creation of Forms of our nature—with all its metamorphoses and symbioses—in monumental paintings that have no equal in contemporary art.* Before the troubling imaginative poverty of a Tanguy, for example, who has been painting the same stony larvae under the same gray sky for twenty-five years, I feel like repeating a phrase that empowered the surrealists of the first wave: *Vous qui ne voyez pas, pensez à ceux qui voient.* There are still too many "adolescents who find pleasure in violating the corpses of newly dead beautiful women" (Lautréamont), unaware of the fact that the truly marvelous would be in violating them while still living. It's just that

---

* Let's observe the American prestige and profound originality that allow the works of Wifredo Lam to stand above those of other artists gathered in the special panoramic issue of *Cahiers d'art*, published in 1946.

too many people forget, by disguising themselves as cheap magicians, that the marvelous begins to exist unequivocally when it surges from an unexpected alteration of reality (the miracle), from a privileged revelation of reality, from an unusual or singularly favorable illumination of the unsung riches of reality, from an amplification of the scales and categories of reality, perceived with particular intensity as a result of an exaltation of the spirit that leads it to a kind of "heightened state." To begin with, the experience of the marvelous presupposes a certain faith. Those who do not believe in saints cannot cure themselves with saintly miracles, just as those who are not Don Quixotes cannot insert themselves body and soul into the world of *Amadís de Gaula* or *Tirant lo Blanc*. Certain statements made by Rutilio in *The Labors of Persiles and Sigismunda* regarding people transformed into wolves would have seemed credible simply because in Cervantes's time it was believed that there were individuals who suffered from lupine mania. In like manner the voyage of the character from Tuscany to Norway on a witch's veil was accepted without question. Marco Polo admitted that certain birds carried elephants in their claws while in flight, and Luther, seeing the devil before him, threw a bottle of ink at his head. Victor Hugo, so exploited by collectors of books about the marvelous, believed in apparitions because he was certain he spoke with [his daughter] Léopoldine's ghost in Guernsey. For Van Gogh it was enough to have faith in the sunflower in order to fix his revelation on canvas. From that point on, the marvelous invoked in disbelief—as was the habit of surrealists for so many years—was nothing more than a literary ruse, as boring in its long life as certain "preconceived" oneiric literature and certain exaltations of madness that are currently very much in vogue. Of course, this is not enough to justify some proponents of a *return to the real*—a term that thus absorbs a gregariously political meaning—who do nothing but substitute the tricks of the prestidigitator for the common figures of the academic writer or the eschatological games of some existentialists. Undoubtedly, little can be offered in defense of the poets and artists who praise sadism without having practiced it, admire the supermacho out of impotence, invoke ghosts without believing that they respond to séances, and found secret societies, literary sects, and vaguely philosophical clubs with saints and signs and arcane ends that are never achieved, and are incapable of conceiving a valid mysticism or abandoning their miserly habits to wager their souls on the one terrifying card of faith.

This became abundantly clear to me during my stay in Haiti as I came in daily contact with something we could call *the marvelous real* [lo real maravilloso]. I was stepping on ground whereon thousands of people eager for freedom believed in the metamorphic powers of Mackandal, to the point where that collective faith would produce a miracle on the day of his execution. I already knew the prodigious story of Bouckman, the Jamaican initiate. I had visited the Citadelle of La Ferrière, a building without architectural precedent, foreshadowed only by the *Imaginary Prisons* of Piranesi. I had breathed the atmosphere created by Henri Christophe, a monarch of remarkable endeavors, which were much more surprising than those of the cruel kings invented by the surrealists, given as they were to imaginary tyrannies although they didn't experience a single one. Every step I took, I came across the marvelous real. Then I thought that the presence and relevance of the marvelous real was not a privilege only of Haiti, but, rather, a patrimony of all of the Americas, where, for example, an accounting of its cosmogonies is yet to be completed. The marvelous real is found every step of the way in the lives of people who inscribed their dates on the history of the continent and left behind surnames still in use: from the seekers of the Fountain of Youth and the golden city of Manoa to the modern heroes of our wars of independence, whose lives became the stuff of myth, such as the female colonel Juana Azurduy. It has always seemed meaningful to me that, in 1780, some sane Spaniards coming out of Angostura [Venezuela] would still throw themselves into the search for El Dorado, and that during the days of the French Revolution—long live Reason and the Supreme Being!—the Compostelan Francisco Menéndez would wander through the lands of Patagonia in search of the City of the Caesars. Shifting our focus to another aspect of the question, we might see, for example, that in contrast to Western European folk dancing, which has lost all magical or incantatory characteristics, rare is the collective dance in the Americas that doesn't embody a deep sense of ritual and create around itself a whole initiating process: thus the dances of Cuban Santeria or the remarkable black version of the Feast of Corpus Christi that can still be seen in the town of San Francisco de Yare, in Venezuela.

In Canto Six of *Maldoror* there is a moment in which the hero, who has been pursued by police the world over, escapes "an army of agents and spies" by transforming himself into different animals and makes use of his gift of traveling instantaneously to Beijing, Madrid, or Saint Petersburg. This is "marvelous literature" in all its glory. But in the Americas, where no such thing was ever written, there was a Mackandal, who was accorded the same powers via the faith of his contemporaries, and using that magic inspired one of the most dramatic and strange rebellions in history. Maldoror—Ducasse himself admits as much—was nothing more than "a poetic Rocambole." Out of him came a short-lived literary school. Out of Mackandal the American, on the other hand, a whole mythology remains, accompanied by magical chants preserved by a whole people and still sung in Vodou ceremonies.* (There is, as well, a strange coincidence in that Isidore Ducasse, a man with a well-developed fantastic-poetic instinct, was born in the Americas and boasted emphatically at the end of one of his cantos of being "*Le Montevidéen.*") It's just that, given its virgin landscape, its formation, its ontology, the Faustian

---

* See Jacques Roumain's *Le sacrifice du tambour-assoto(r)*.

presence of the Indian and the black, the revolution brought about by its recent discovery, and the fecund racial mixtures it enabled, the Americas are far from exhausting their mythological riches.

Without having proposed it in a systematic way, the text that follows has responded to these types of concerns. It contains the narrative of a series of extraordinary events that transpired on the island of Saint-Domingue, in a span of time briefer than that of a human life, letting the marvelous flow freely from a reality fully described in all its details. Here I am compelled to state that the story you are about to read rests on a foundation of extremely rigorous research that not only respects the true sequence of events, the names of characters, including secondary ones, and of places and even streets, but also hides, outside of time though it is, an exacting concern for the dates and chronology of these events. Nevertheless, the dramatic uniqueness of these happenings and the fantastic composure of characters who found themselves at a certain moment in the magical crossroads of the city of the Cap result in a marvelous story that couldn't possibly be set in Europe and, moreover, is as real as any event included in schoolbooks for the edification of young readers. But what is the story of all of the Americas if not the chronicle of the marvelous and the real?

—A.C.
(translated by Pablo Medina)

PART ONE

THE DEVIL:

    I demand permission to enter . . .

PROVIDENCE:

    Who is it?

THE DEVIL:

    The King of the West.

PROVIDENCE:

    I know you, oh cursed one. Come in.

(*He enters.*)

THE DEVIL:

    Oh, holy tribunal,
    eternal Providence,
    where are you sending Columbus
    to renew my evil work?
    Don't you know that for many years
    I've had possession of those lands?

—Lope de Vega

1

Wax Heads

Of the twenty stallions brought to Cap Français by a boat captain who was somewhat of a middleman for a Norman breeder, Ti Noël quickly picked out a white-footed stud horse with a rounded croup he knew would be good for mating with mares that were producing increasingly smaller foals. Monsieur Lenormand de Mézy, confident of the slave's expertise in equine matters, did not think twice and paid the price in ringing gold coins. After making a bridle out of rope, Ti Noël appreciated the full breadth of the solid, mottled beast between his thighs, feeling the soapy sweat that soon turned to foam on the Percheron's thick hide. As he followed his master, who rode a chestnut with a quicker step, the slave passed the neighborhood of the sea folk, with warehouses redolent of brine, sails thickened by dampness, and hardtack that had to be broken apart with a blow of the fist, before coming to the main street, which was brightened at that hour of the morning by the vivid colors of the head scarves of domestic slave women returning from market. As the governor's carriage passed, festooned with gilded decorations, Monsieur Lenormand de Mézy gave a full salute. Then the slave and his master tied their mounts in front of the barbershop, whose owner subscribed to the *Leyden Gazette* for the entertainment of his cultured patrons.

While his master was being shaved, Ti Noël was able to study carefully the four wax heads propped on the shelf by the entrance. The wigs' curls framed the fixed faces before spreading into a pool of ringlets on the red runner. Those heads seemed as real—and as dead, given their motionless eyes—as the talking head that a traveling charlatan had brought to the Cap years before as a ploy to help him sell an elixir that cured toothaches and rheumatism. By charming coincidence, the butcher shop next door displayed the skinned heads of calves, which had the same waxy quality. Sporting a sprig of parsley on the tongue, they seemed asleep among scarlet oxtails, hooves in gelatin, and pots of stewed tripe in the mode of Caen. Only a wooden partition separated the counters, and Ti Noël distracted himself by thinking that the heads of white gentlemen were being served at the same table as the discolored veal heads. Just as fowl were adorned with their feathers when served to diners at a banquet, so it seemed that an expert and rather grotesque chef had dressed the human heads with the most gloriously arranged wigs. All they needed was a bed of lettuce or radishes cut in the shape of fleurs-de-lys as adornment. Furthermore, the containers of gum arabic, the bottles of lavender cologne, and the boxes of rice powder near the pots of innards and trays of kidneys completed, along with other jars and bottles, the mise-en-scène of an abominable feast.

There was an abundance of heads that morning. Next to the butcher shop, the bookseller had hung along a wire the latest prints he'd received from Paris. At least four of them depicted the face of the king of France, framed by suns, swords, and laurel branches. But there were many other wigged heads, probably belonging to important persons of the court. The warriors could be identified by their warlike gestures; the magistrates by their threatening countenance; the ingenious writers because they appeared smiling with their sharpened plumes hovering over verses that said nothing to Ti Noël, since slaves knew nothing of letters. There were also etchings in color, less serious in nature, depicting fireworks celebrating the taking of a city, scenes of doctors dancing with huge syringes in their hands, a game of blindman's buff in a park, libertine young men putting their hands inside the necklines of chambermaids, and the inevitable shrewdness of a lover lying enraptured on the grass while spying the undergarments of a lady moving innocently back and forth on a swing. But Ti Noël was drawn at that moment by a copper etching, the last of the series, which was different from the rest in its theme and execution. It depicted what appeared to be an admiral or French ambassador being received by a black man surrounded by feather fans and seated on a throne adorned by the figures of monkeys and lizards.

"Who is that?" he asked the bookseller, who was lighting a large clay pipe on the threshold of his store.

"He is the king of your country."

The young slave hardly needed confirmation of what he was already thinking, since he quickly remembered the stories Mackandal told at the sugar mill during those hours when the oldest horse in Lenormand de Mézy's plantation made the cylinders turn. Feigning a tired voice to enhance the effects of certain key parts, the Mandingo would refer to events that had occurred during the reigns of Popo, Arada, the Nagos and the Fulas. He spoke of vast migrations of people, of secular wars, of huge battles in which the animals had helped the humans. He knew the story of Adonhueso, of the king of Angola, of King Dá, the incarnation of the Snake (eternal beginning that never ends), who spent his time in mystical consort with a queen who was the rainbow, lady of the waters and of birth. And he went on with interminable stories about the feats of Kankán Muza, the fierce Muza, creator of the invincible Mandingo empire, whose horses were adorned with silver coins and embroidered blankets, whinnying over the clash of irons and bringing thunder in the skin of two drums hanging from a cross. Furthermore, those kings, made invulnerable through the science of their priests, marched at the heads of their armies holding their lances and would be wounded only if they had somehow offended the Gods of

Thunder or the Gods of the Forge. Kings they were, true kings, and not those sovereigns covered with someone else's hair, who played lawn games and only knew how to be gods in the theatrics of the court, showing their girlish legs to the rhythm of a rigadoon. Those white sovereigns rarely heard the roar of cannons firing over the spur of a half-moon. More common to their ears were the violins of symphonies, the hurdy-gurdies of libel, the gossip of their mistresses, and the songs of their windup birds. Although his lights were meager, Ti Noël had gathered these truths from Mackandal's deep well of knowledge. In Africa the king was warrior, hunter, judge, and priest; his precious seed swelled hundreds of wombs with a vigorous caste of heroes. In France and Spain, on the other hand, the king sent his generals into battle; he was incapable of settling litigation; he allowed himself to be upbraided by a lowly friar confessor; and, as far as his seed was concerned, he couldn't engender anything but a weakling prince, incapable of finishing off a deer without the help of his huntsmen, who referred to the boy, with unconscious irony, by the name of an inoffensive and frivolous fish called the dolphin. On the other hand, over there—the *Great Over There*—were princes hard as anvils and princes who were leopards and princes who knew the language of the trees and princes who ruled over the four cardinal points, owners of cloud, seed, bronze, and fire.

Ti Noël heard the voice of his master, who was leaving the barbershop with too much rice powder on his cheeks. His face now bore a surprising resemblance to the four wax faces that were lined along the shelf, smiling stupidly. On his way, Monsieur Lenormand de Mézy bought a calf's head in the butcher shop and gave it to the slave to carry. Mounted on the seed stallion, which was now eager to reach the pasture, Ti Noël felt the cold white skull, thinking it might resemble the shape of the bald head of his master hidden under his wig. Meanwhile, the street had filled with people. But instead of black women returning from market, now there were ladies coming from ten o'clock mass. More than one quadroon woman, the companion of a wealthy administrator or other, would be followed by a servant of the same uncertain color as she, carrying for her a palm frond fan, a breviary, and a parasol with gilded tassels. At a street corner a crowd watched a puppet show. Farther on, a sailor tried to sell to the ladies a small monkey from Brazil dressed in Spanish clothes. In the taverns, barkeeps opened bottles of wine cooled in barrels of salt and wet sand. Father Cornejo, a priest from Limonade, had just arrived at the main church, mounted on a mule the color of an ass.

Monsieur Lenormand de Mézy and his slave left the city along a road that bordered the sea. A cannonade from high atop the fortress greeted *La Courageuse*, of the king's royal navy, which had just appeared on the horizon on its return from Île de la Tortue. The ship's cannons echoed back a white roar. Overcome by memories of his time as an impoverished officer, the master began whistling an old fife march. Ti Noël, in mental counterpoint, hummed to himself a sailor's song, popular among the coopers of the port, about hurling shit at the king of England. He was certain of it, even though the words were not in Kreyol. He knew the song. Besides, the king of England was the same to him as the king of France or of Spain, who ruled the other side of the island, and whose women—as Mackandal had it—reddened their cheeks with bull's blood and buried fetuses in a convent basement filled with skeletons that were refused entry into a heaven that did not accept the dead unacquainted with the true gods.

2

The Pruning

Ti Noël was sitting on an upended tub, letting the old horse turn the sugar mill at a pace made perfectly regular from habit. Mackandal grabbed the sugarcane in bundles, shoving one end through the iron cylinders. With his blood-shot eyes, his powerful torso, and his small waist, the Mandingo exerted a strange fascination over Ti Noël. It was a known fact that his deep, deafening voice got him whatever he wanted from the negresses. His gifts as a narrator and his wild gestures as he described his charac-ters made the men stand silent, especially when he re-ferred to the trip he took as a captive years before being sold to the slave dealers of Sierra Leone. Hearing him, the young man understood that Cap Français, with its bell towers, its stone buildings, and its Norman houses pro-tected from the sun by long-roofed balconies, was nothing compared with the cities of Guinea, where there were clay cupolas that rose over large fortresses surrounded by battle-ments and markets that were known beyond the edges of the desert and beyond the landless towns. The artisans of those cities were experts at softening metals, forging swords that cut like razor blades and were light as wings in the hands of warriors. Powerful rivers, born in ice, lapped the feet of men, and it was not necessary to bring salt from the Country of Salt. There were large buildings that housed wheat, sesame seed, and millet and there was commerce between kingdoms that included the olive oil and wines of Andalusia. Gigantic drums slept under palm frond blankets, mother drums, with legs painted red and human figures depicted on them. The rains obeyed the incantations of the wise men, and during the feasts of circumcision, when adolescents danced with their thighs smeared in blood, wood slabs were struck producing a sound like that of large domesticated waterfalls. In the sacred city of Widah the cobra was worshipped as the mystical representation of the eternal ring, as were gods who ruled over the vegetable kingdom and appeared colorful and resplendent amid bulrushes that grew placidly along the shores of salt lakes.

The exhausted horse fell on its knees. There was a sound so long and disturbing that it spread over the neighboring plantations and scattered the pigeons. Caught by the cylinders that had lurched forward with unexpected suddenness, Mackandal's left hand had moved with the cane, pulling the arm in to the shoulder. An eye of blood widened in the container of sugarcane juice. Ti Noël grabbed a knife and cut the reins that tied the horse to the mill pole. The tannery slaves rushed to the mill, running behind their master. Workers came, too, from the kitchen and cocoa dryers. Mackandal pulled his mangled arm, making the cylinders move in reverse. With his right hand he tried to move the elbow and wrist that had stopped responding to his commands. He had a stupefied look in his eyes. They began to tighten a tourniquet of rope around the armpit to stanch the hemorrhage. The master ordered someone to bring a sharpening stone to hone the machete for the amputation.

3

What the Hand Discovered

No longer fit for hard labor, Mackandal was sent to herd cattle. He brought the herd out of the stables before dawn and took it to the mountain's shady side where a thick pasture grew that held the dew well into morning. As he observed the slow spread of the animals grazing over the tall carpet of clover, he noticed that they ignored certain plants. Lying under the shade of a carob tree, he leaned on the elbow of his healthy arm and searched the familiar grasses with his hand, looking for those weeds he might have previously ignored. He was surprised to learn the secret life of unique plant species, given to disguise, confusion, and the greenest of greens, friends to the little armored creatures that avoided the ant paths. The hand picked unknown canary grasses, sulfurous capers, minuscule peppers, vines that wove nets in between stones; solitary plants with downy leaves that sweated at night; sensitives that closed at the mere sound of the human voice; capsules that burst at midday with the sound a fingernail makes when popping a flea; and creeping lianas that clustered away from the sun in frothing tangles. There was a vine that stung the skin and another that made the head of whoever rested in its shade swell. But Mackandal was even more interested in mushrooms. Mushrooms that smelled of wood rot, flasks, basements, and illness, and pricked the ears and tongues of cattle; others with wrinkled flesh that covered themselves in excretions or opened their striped umbrellas in cold hollows where toads stared or slept without blinking. The Mandingo broke apart the meat of a mushroom with his fingers, bringing it to his nose and smelling poison. Then he made a cow smell his hand. When the beast snorted and turned its head away with fear in its eyes, Mackandal gathered more mushrooms of the same species, storing them in an uncured leather bag that hung from his neck.

Under pretext of bathing the horses, Ti Noël would visit Mackandal and spend hours away from Lenormand de Mézy's plantation. Together they walked to the edge of the valley, where the land became uneven and the base of the mountain had been eroded into deep crevices. They stopped at the home of an old woman who lived alone, even though she was regularly visited by people from far away. Various sabers hung from the wall among red flags draped from heavy poles, horseshoes, meteorites, and loops of wire on which dangled moldy spoons in the shape of a cross to scare off Baron Samedi, Baron Piquant, Baron La Croix, and other lords of the cemetery. Mackandal showed Maman Loi the leaves, grasses, mushrooms, and samples he'd brought in his bag. She examined them carefully, squeezing and smelling some and throwing others away. Sometimes they spoke of egregious animals that were part human. And also of people who had acquired lycanthropic powers as a result of certain spells. There were stories of women raped by large cats that had exchanged at night the roar for the word. One time Maman Loi became strangely mute just before the best part of a story. Reacting to a mysterious command, she ran to the kitchen and sank her arms into a pot of boiling oil. Ti Noël noticed that her face reflected a terse indifference, and what was even stranger, when she pulled her arms out of the oil, there were no blisters or any other sign of burns despite the horrible frying sound he'd just heard. Since Mackandal seemed to accept the matter with absolute calm, Ti Noël made an effort to hide his astonishment. And the conversation between the Mandingo and the witch continued placidly, with long pauses when they both looked off into the distance.

One day they caught a dog in heat that belonged to Lenormand de Mézy's pack. While Ti Noël stood over it holding it by the ears, Mackandal rubbed its snout with a stone dyed yellow by the juice of a mushroom. The dog's muscles went into spasms. Almost immediately its body was shaken by violent convulsions. It fell on its back with its legs stiff and its teeth bared. That afternoon, when they returned to the plantation, Mackandal stopped for some time to study the mills, the cocoa and coffee dryers, the washroom, the forge, the cisterns, and the ovens.

"The time has come," he said.

The next day they called him in vain. The master organized a search party, simply to set an example for the blacks, even though he didn't put much effort into it. A one-armed slave was of little value. Besides, it was well-known that every Mandingo hid in him a potential runaway. To say "Mandingo" was to say rebellious, unruly, demonic. That's why people from those regions of Africa were worth so little in the markets. They all dreamed of escaping into the wild. But with so many properties abutting each other, it was doubtful the runaway would get very far. When he was returned to the plantation, he'd be punished in front of the rest, as a warning. A one-armed man was nothing more than that. It would be foolish to run the risk of losing a couple of good mastiffs if Mackandal tried to silence them with a machete.

4

The Account

Ti Noël was deeply saddened by Mackandal's disappearance. Had he been asked, he would have accepted gladly the role of serving the Mandingo. Now he imagined that the one-armed slave thought so little of him he wouldn't make him an accomplice to his projects. During those long nights when the young man was upset about being left behind, he rose from the manger in which he slept and embraced the neck of the Norman stud horse, weeping and burying his face in its warm mane, which smelled freshly washed. Mackandal's departure was also the departure of the world evoked by his stories. Kankán Muza, Adonhueso, the royal kings, and Widah's rainbow had also left with him. With the spice of life gone, Ti Noël was bored by Sunday celebrations, instead spending his time caring for the beasts, whose ears and perineums he always kept free of ticks. In this fashion the rainy season passed.

One day, when the river waters receded, Ti Noël ran into the old woman of the mountain in the vicinity of the stables. She was bringing him a message from Mackandal. And so, as dawn spread, the young man entered the narrow opening of a cavern filled with stalagmites, which descended into a deeper cavity covered with bats hanging by their legs. The ground was carpeted with a thick layer of guano that trapped corroded objects and petrified fish bones. Ti Noël noticed that a number of clay jars occupied the center. A bitter, heavy smell spread from them into the damp gloom. A mound of lizard skins lay on a surface of banana leaves. A large flagstone and several round and flat stones had been used recently, it was obvious, in a process of maceration. On a tree trunk, which had been smoothed out along its length, was a ledger stolen from the plantation's bookkeeper. Its pages were covered with signs drawn roughly in charcoal. Ti Noël could only think of the botanical stores of the Cap, with their large mortars, their recipe books resting on lecterns, their jars of nux vomica and asafetida, and their bunches of marshmallow root for curing gum disease. The only things missing were scorpions in alcohol, roses in oil, and tanks for breeding leeches.

Mackandal had grown thin. His muscles now slid directly over his bones, sculpting his torso into a lithe shape. But his countenance, which took on an olive hue by the light of the lamp, exuded a quiet joy. What most surprised Ti Noël was the revelation of the long and patient labor the Mandingo had accomplished since the night of his escape. It seemed that he had gone to each and every plantation of the Plaine and established direct relationships with those who worked in them. He knew, for example, that in the indigo processing room of Dondón he could count on Olain the gardener, on Romaine the cook of the barracks, and on the one-eyed Jean-Pierrot; in the plantation of Lenormand de Mézy he had sent messages to the three Pongé brothers, to the new Congos, to the bowlegged Fula, and to Marinette, the mulatto woman who had in previous times slept in the bed of the master before being returned to the indigo processing room upon the arrival of a certain Mademoiselle de la Martinière, who was married off to the master in absentia in a convent in Le Havre before sailing for the colony. He had also gotten in touch with the two Angolans who were hiding on the other side of the Bonnet à l'Évêque and whose striped behinds preserved the evidence of red-hot irons applied as punishment for stealing rum. With characters only he could decipher, Mackandal had recorded in his registry the name of the bocor of Milot, and even of the guides who would be of help in leading groups across the cordillera and establishing contact with the people of Artibonite.

Ti Noël found out that day what the One-Armed Man expected from him. That same Sunday, when he returned from mass, the master learned that the two best milk cows in the plantation—the white-tailed ones brought from Rouen—were lying in their own feces near death, vomiting bile through their snouts. Ti Noël explained to him that the animals brought from distant countries were prone to mistaking the grass they ate, sometimes taking for delicious treats certain shoots that poisoned their blood.

5

De Profundis

The poison spread through the Plaine du Nord, invading pastures and stables. No one knew how it advanced among the grass and the alfalfa, how it was introduced into bales of hay, or how it crawled up into the mangers. The fact was that cows, oxen, calves, horses, and sheep burst open by the hundreds, covering the region with the ubiquitous stench of carrion. At dusk great fires were lit that gave off a base, greasy smell before dying out over mounds of bovine skulls, carbonized rib cages, and hooves reddened by the flames. The most accomplished herbalists of the Cap searched in vain for the leaf, the resin, or the sap that might have brought such devastation. The beasts kept dropping, their bellies swollen, covered by buzzing green flies. Large black birds with bald heads waited on the roofs for the moment when they could let themselves drop and break through the distended hides with their beaks, releasing even more of the pestilence.

It was soon learned, with horror, that the poison had

entered the homes. One afternoon, after snacking on a sweet bun, the owner of the plantation of Coq-Chante had fallen suddenly, without previous signs of illness, bringing down with him a wall clock he was winding. Before the news could reach neighboring plantations, other owners died from the poison, which lay in wait, crouching as if to strike more effectively, in soup tureens, medicine bottles, bread, wine, fruit, and salt. The sinister hammering of coffins sounded by the hour. Around every turn of the road a funeral appeared. The only prayer heard in the churches of the Cap was the Office of the Dead, and the extreme unction arrived always too late, accompanied by distant bells that tolled for the newly dead. The priests had to quicken their Latin to attend to all the mourning families. The same funerary prayer sounded throughout the Plaine, bringing with it the lugubrious tones of the great hymn of terror, which tightened throats and thinned out faces. Under the shade of silver crosses that came and went along the roads, the green poison, the yellow poison, or the poison that had no color kept slithering in, going down kitchen chimneys or sneaking through the cracks of closed doors, like an uncontainable snaking vine that might turn bodies into shadows. Hour after hour the sinister refrains of the cantors moved from the Miserere to the De Profundis.

Exasperated by fear, inebriated with wine they drank instead of well water, the planters whipped and tortured their slaves, searching for an explanation. But the poison kept decimating families and destroying people and animals despite the prayers, the medical advice, the promises to saints, or the useless remedies of a Breton sailor, who was a necromancer and quack. Nothing could stop the subterranean march of death. In an unwitting hurry to occupy the last grave remaining in the cemetery, Madame Lenormand de Mézy passed away on Pentecost Sunday a short time after tasting a particularly appealing orange that an all-too-complacent branch had placed within easy reach of her hands. A state of siege was proclaimed on the Plaine. Anyone wandering the fields or in the vicinity of the houses after dusk was brought down by musket shot without warning. The garrison at the Cap had marched through the roads in a comical attempt to threaten an invisible enemy. But the poison kept reaching mouths in the most unexpected ways. One day the eight Du Periguy family members were found in a vat of cider they themselves had carried from the hold of a newly anchored ship. Carrion took over the whole region.

One afternoon when he was threatened with a load of gunpowder up his behind, a bowlegged Fula wound up talking. The one-armed Mackandal, who had been made a Vodou priest in the Rada rite and was invested with extraordinary powers through various spells under the grace of the greater gods, was the Lord of Poison. Given supreme authority by the chiefs from the other shore, he had been elected to proclaim the crusade of extermination against whites and create a great empire of free blacks in Saint-

Domingue. He had thousands of slaves as followers. Nobody could now stop the march of the poison. That revelation raised a storm of complaints in the plantations. And no sooner had the gunpowder, lit out of pure wrath, exploded in the intestines of the squealing slave, than a messenger was dispatched to the Cap. That same afternoon all available men were recruited to hunt down Mackandal. The Plaine—reeking of green flesh, half-burned hooves, and the labor of worms—filled with dog barks and blasphemies.

6

The Metamorphosis

During several weeks the soldiers from the garrison at the Cap and patrols consisting of planters, accountants, and overseers searched the region, copse after copse, ravine after ravine, thicket after thicket, without finding a trace of Mackandal. Once its source was discovered, however, the poison stopped its offensive, retreating to the clay pots that the One-Armed Man must have buried somewhere, turning to foam in the great night of the earth that had already engulfed so many lives. The dogs and the men returned from the forest at dusk, sweating exhaustion and spite out of every pore. Now that death had gone back to its normal rhythms, at a time when people suffered only the slight colds of January or certain peculiar fevers awakened by the rains, the planters took to drinking and gambling, corrupted as they were by having to live alongside common soldiers. Amid obscene songs and cheating schemes, they grabbed the breasts of the negresses as they passed bringing fresh glasses, and they recounted the feats of

grandfathers who had taken part in the looting of Carta-
gena de Indias or had sunk their hands into the treasure
of the Spanish crown when Peg-Leg Piet Hein accomplished the fabulous feat dreamed of by corsairs for nearly
two decades. Over tables stained with strong wine, between
one throw of the dice and another, they offered toasts to
d'Esnambuc, Bertrand d'Ogeron, Du Rausset, and the men
of true courage who had created the colony at their own
risk and expense, making the law by the seat of their britches
without ever being intimidated by edicts printed in Paris
or by the bland counterclaims of the Black Code. Asleep
under the stairways, the hounds rested free of their leashes.

The searches for Mackandal became less frequent.
They were undertaken now with great lassitude, inter-
spersed with picnics and siestas under the shade of trees.
Several months passed without news of the One-Armed
Man. Some believed he had sought refuge in the cloud-
covered heights of the Plateau in the center of the country,
where the blacks danced fandangos with castanets. Others
maintained that the Vodou priest was taken by schooner
to the Jacmel region and was operating there, where many
dead men worked the land as long as they were never fed
salt. Nevertheless, the slaves were in defiant good humor.
Those in charge of sounding out rhythms for the milling
of corn or the cutting of sugarcane had never beaten their
drums with such enthusiasm. At night in their barracks
and huts, the blacks told one another the strangest news
with great joy: a green iguana was seen warming itself on

the roof of the tobacco barn; someone had seen a nocturnal butterfly flying at midday; a large dog with bristled hair had raced across the house, stealing a deer leg; a gannet had shaken its wings and dropped its lice on the vine trellis of the backyard.

Everyone knew that the green iguana, the nocturnal butterfly, the stray dog, and the fantastic gannet were nothing but simple disguises. Graced with the power to transform himself into cloven-hoofed animals, birds, fish, or insects, Mackandal often visited the plantations of the Plaine to watch over the faithful and learn if they still believed in his return. From one metamorphosis to the next, the One-Armed Man was everywhere, having recovered his physical shape by dressing in animal garb. With wings one day, gills the next, galloping or crawling, he had become lord of the subterranean rivers, the coastal caves, the treetops, and he reigned over the whole island. Now his powers were limitless. He could mount a mare or rest in the coolness of a cistern, perch on the small branches of an acacia or slip through a keyhole; he changed his shadow according to his will. By his own doing a negress gave birth to a child with the face of a wild boar. At night he appeared on the roads in the shape of a black goat with embers on his horns. One day he would give the sign for the great uprising, and the Lords from Over There, led by Damballah, by the Master of the Roads, and by Ogun of the Metals, would bring the lightning and thunder and unleash the hurricane that would complete the labor men had begun. "In that great hour," Ti Noël said, "the blood of the whites will run in the streams, where the *loas*, inebriated with joy, will lie facedown and drink it until they are full."

Four years they waited anxiously, and their alert ears refused to despair of not hearing, at any moment, the sound of the large conch shells that would blow in the mountains to announce that Mackandal had closed the cycle of his metamorphoses, standing once more on his manly legs, muscled and hard, with testicles like stones.

7

In Human Dress

After sending Marinette the laundress back to her room for a time, Monsieur Lenormand de Mézy was married again, in a match arranged by the priest of Limonade, to a lame, devout, and rich widow. And so, when the first storms of that December blew, the domestic slaves of the house, directed by the mistress's cane, began to place Provençal *santons* around a grotto made of brown paper, still redolent of warm glue, destined to be lit up at Christmas under the eaves of the porch. Toussaint the woodworker had carved some wise men that were too large for the tableau and were never included, especially because of the oversized, fearsome white corneas of Balthasar—particularly enhanced with fresh paint—that seemed to emerge from the ebony night with the terrified look of a drowned man. Ti Noël and the other slaves helped out with the construction of the Nativity scene, aware that the days of Christmas bonuses and midnight masses were soon approaching, and that their masters' parties and celebrations would make them relax their discipline somewhat, to the point that it was not difficult to steal a pig's ear from the kitchen or take a mouthful from the tap of a wine cask or sneak at night into the barracks of the newly bought Angolan women, whom the master would enjoy under Christian sacrament after the holidays. But this time Ti Noël knew he wouldn't be around when the candles were lit and the gilt walls of the grotto would shine. He intended to be far away that night, escaping to the festivities organized by the slaves of the Dufrené plantation, who had been authorized to celebrate the birth of the first male of the master's household with one mug of Spanish brandy per person.

Roulé, roulé, Congoa roulé!
Roulé, roulé, Congoa roulé!
A fort ti fille ya dansé congo ya-ya-ró!

For more than two hours the drum hides thundered by the light of the torches and the women repeated their rhythmic clothes-washing gestures, when a commotion made the voices of the singers tremble. Behind the Mother Drum, the human visage of Mackandal rose. Mackandal the Mandingo. Mackandal the Man, the One-Armed Man. Restored. In the flesh. No one greeted him, but his eyes met everyone's. And the mugs of brandy began to pass from hand to hand toward the one hand that had the greatest thirst. Ti Noël saw him for the first time since the metamorphosis. Something remained in him as a result of hiding in mysterious places: scales, pelt, fleece. His beard was sharp and long and feline; his eyes spread out toward the temples, like those of the birds whose appearance he used as disguise. Women passed continually in front of him, shaking their hips to the rhythms of the dance. But there were so many questions in the atmosphere that, suddenly, without warning, all the voices joined in a solemn chant that drowned out the percussion. After a four-year wait, the song became the vehicle for an infinite number of complaints:

Yenvalo moin Papa!
Moin pas mangé q'm bambó
Yenvalou, Papa, yenvalou moin!
Ou vlai moin lavé chaudier;
Yenvalo moin?

Will I have to wash the pots forever? Will I have to eat bamboo forever? As if coming from the gut, the questions came tightly together, gathering in choir form, a wail torn from the peoples driven into exile to build mausoleums, towers, and endless walls. Oh Father, my father, how long is the road! Oh Father, my father, how long the sorrow! Because of all the lamentations, Ti Noël forgot that the whites, too, had ears. That's why, in the courtyard of the Dufrené house, the muskets, blunderbusses, and pistols were taken from their display cases in the salon and loaded with gunshot. And in case they were needed, knives, rapiers, and clubs were left in reserve under the care of the women, who had already started their prayers asking for the capture of the Mandingo.

8

The Great Flight

On a Monday in January just before dawn, groups from the Plaine du Nord began entering the city of the Cap. Led by their masters and overseers on horseback and escorted by heavily armed guards, the slaves gradually turned the central plaza black as the military snare drums sounded a solemn beat. Several soldiers gathered bundles of firewood at the foot of a quebracho pole, while others stoked the flames of a fire pit. In the atrium of the major parish church, next to the governor, the judges, and the king's officers, the authorities from the capital sat on tall red chairs under a funeral awning hanging from poles and struts. In the balconies small parasols moved like colorful arrangements of flowers on a windowsill. Ladies with fans and gloves chatted loudly as if from the box seats of a theater, their voices delighted by the excitement. Those whose windows looked out over the plaza had lemonade and almond drinks prepared for their guests. Below, the blacks were increasingly packed together, sweating and expecting a spectacle prepared especially for them: a gala function for blacks with no expense spared. This time the message would enter with fire and not with blood, and very expensive festival lights were lit in such a way that it would not be forgotten.

Suddenly all the fans closed at the same time and the snare drums grew silent. Wearing torn pants, covered with knotted ropes, and showing fresh wounds on his body, Mackandal moved toward the center of the plaza. The masters looked intently at the faces of their slaves but the blacks showed a disarming lack of interest. What did whites know about black matters? In his cycle of metamorphoses, Mackandal had entered into the hidden world of insects, countering the loss of his arm by acquiring several legs or four wings or long antennae. He'd been a fly, a centipede, a moth, a termite, a tarantula, a ladybug, and even a firefly glowing with large green lights. At the right moment, the ropes around the Mandingo, now loose around his body, would draw for a moment the outline of a man made of air, before slipping down the length of the pole. And the Mandingo, transformed into a buzzing mosquito, would go to rest on the tricorn of the captain of the troop to better enjoy the bewilderment of the whites. That's what the masters ignored; that's why they had wasted so much money in organizing this useless spectacle, which would reveal their impotence in fighting a man anointed by the Great Loas.

Mackandal was now tied to the pole. The executioner

grabbed an ember with tongs. Repeating a gesture he had perfected the previous night before the mirror, the governor unsheathed his sword and gave the order for the sentence to be served. The fire began to ascend toward the One-Armed Man and singed his legs. At that moment Mackandal shook the stump of his arm in a threatening gesture, which, though diminished, was no less terrifying, wailing out unknown curses and stretching his torso violently forward. His ties fell and the black man's body shot up into the air, flying overhead before disappearing into the black masses of slaves. Only one scream filled the plaza.

"Mackandal sauvé!"

All was confusion and chaos. The guards threw themselves at the wailing crowd, hitting them with their gun butts. The crowd no longer seemed to fit amid the houses and climbed toward the balconies. And the noise and screaming and the mob was such that few saw that Mackandal, held down by ten soldiers, was being forced head-first into the fire and that a flame enhanced by his burning hair drowned out his last scream. When the groups calmed down, the fire burned normally, like any fire made with good wood, and the breeze coming from the ocean lifted thick smoke toward the balconies, where more than one fainted lady was coming to. There was nothing left to see.

That afternoon the slaves returned to their plantations, laughing the whole way. Mackandal had fulfilled his promise to remain in the kingdom of this world. Once again the whites had been mocked by the Great Powers from the Other Shore. And while Monsieur Lenormand de Mézy, wearing his sleeping cap, made a comment to his saintly wife about the insensibility of the blacks before the suffering of one of their own—reaching some philosophical conclusions regarding the inequality of the races that he hoped to develop into a speech laced with Latin phrases—Ti Noël got one of the kitchen slaves pregnant with twins after sticking her three times in one of the mangers of the horse stable.

PART TWO

. . . je lui dis qu'elle serait reine là-bas, qu'elle irait en palanquin, qu'une esclave serait attentive au moindre de ses mouvements pour exécuter sa volonté, qu'elle se promènerait sous des orangers en fleur, que les serpents ne devaient lui faire aucune peur, attendu qu'il n'y en avait pas dans les Antilles, que les sauvages n'étaient pas plus à craindre, que ce n'était pas là que la broche était mise pour rôtir les gens. Enfin j'achevai mon discours de consolation en lui disant qu'elle serait bien jolie, mise à la créole.

I told her she would be queen there, that she would travel around in a palanquin, that a slave would be at her disposal at all times to satisfy her merest wish, that she would walk about under orange blossoms, that she wouldn't need to be afraid of snakes as there were none in the Antilles, that the savages were not to be feared, that people were not roasted on spits there. Finally, I concluded by saying that she would look very nice dressed as a Creole.

—Madame d'Abrantès

1

The Daughter of Minos
and Pasiphaë

Soon after the death of Monsieur Lenormand de Mézy's second wife, Ti Noël had the opportunity to go to the Cap to pick up some ceremonial harnesses ordered from Paris. During those years the city had progressed remarkably. Almost all the houses had two floors with wide overhanging eaves and tall arched doors, decorated with polished squared bolts or trefoil hinges. There were more tailors, hatters, feather sellers, and wigmakers. One store sold violas and transverse flutes, as well as scores for contredanses and sonatas. The bookseller exhibited the latest issue of the *Gazette de Saint-Domingue*, printed on thin paper, with the text framed by vignettes and half leads. To pile luxury on top of luxury, a theater for opera and dramatic works had been inaugurated on Vaudreuil Street. The prosperity especially favored the Street of the Spaniards, leading the wealthier foreigners to stay at Pension La Couronne, which Henri Christophe, the master chef, had just bought from its previous owner, Mademoiselle Monjeon. The black man's stews were praised for their perfect seasoning by clients newly arrived from Paris; and his *ollas podridas* for the abundance of vegetables, whenever he had to satisfy the appetite of a well-heeled Spaniard, of the sort who came from the other side of the island dressed in such outmoded clothes that they looked like ancient buccaneers. It was also true that Henri Christophe, wearing a tall chef's hat and surrounded by the steam of the kitchen, had a special gift for baking turtle vols-au-vent or sautéing ringdoves on high heat. When it came to the kneading trough, he was capable of baking regal pastries, the aroma of which spread beyond the Street of the Three Faces.

Once again alone, Monsieur Lenormand de Mézy did not have the least respect for the memory of his deceased wife and went with increasing frequency to the Theater of the Cap, where actresses from Paris sang arias by Jean-Jacques Rousseau or recited nobly tragic alexandrines, wiping sweat from their faces while marking a hemistich. Around that time a libelous, anonymous poem complaining about the inconstancy of certain widowers revealed to everyone that a rich owner of the Plaine was amusing himself at night with the bountiful Flemish beauty of a certain Mademoiselle Floridor, a poor actress in the role of confidante, who was always forced to hide in the chorus but was skilled like few in the fellatious arts. Suddenly she had decided at the end of a season that the master should go to Paris, leaving the administration of the plantation in the hands of a relative. But something quite surprising happened to him: after a few months, a growing nostalgia for sun, for space, for abundance, for dominion, and for black women lying on the edges of a pasture revealed to him that the "return to France" for which he'd been working all these years was no longer the key to his happiness. And after so many curses against the colony, so many complaints about its climate, so much criticism of the rudeness of the adventure-seeking settlers, he had returned to his plantation, bringing with him the actress, who'd been rejected by the theaters of Paris because of her meager dramatic talent. That is why on Sundays, two magnificent coaches with postillions in fine livery once again adorned the Plaine on their way to the main church. Dominating the sedan of Mademoiselle Floridor—the actress insisted on being called by her theatrical name—ten restless mulatto women in blue petticoats sat in the back and twittered as loudly as they could in a great fuss of females blown by the wind.

Twenty years passed. Ti Noël fathered twelve children with one of the cooks. The plantation was more prosperous than ever, its roads bordered by ipecac shrubs and its grapevines already producing a premature bitter wine. Nevertheless, as he grew older, Monsieur Lenormand de Mézy had turned into a maniac and a drunk. A constant pathological eroticism had him stalking the adolescent slave girls whose smell and color drove him wild. He was increasingly given to handing out bodily punishment to the men, especially when he found them having sex outside of marriage. For her part, the actress, haggard and ill with

malaria, sought vengeance for her artistic failure by whip-
ping for the merest offense the negresses who bathed and
combed her. Some nights she would drink. Then it was not
unusual for her to awaken the whole crew, the moon already high in the sky, to declaim in front of the slaves, in
between loud burps of malmsey wine, the great roles she'd
never had a chance to interpret. Dressed in the veils of a
confidante or a shy woman in a procession, she attacked
with her broken voice the high-flown pieces of repertory
bravura:

> *Mes crimes désormais ont comblé la mesure:*
> *Je respire à la fois l'inceste et l'imposture;*
> *Mes homicides mains, promptes à me venger,*
> *Dans le sang innocent brûlent de se plonger.*

Dumbfounded and unable to understand anything, yet
also recognizing words that in Kreyol referred to offenses
carrying punishments such as beatings or decapitation,
the blacks came to believe that the lady must have commit-
ted many crimes in her previous life and was in the colony
probably to escape the Paris police, like so many prostitutes of the Cap, who had outstanding warrants back in
the metropolis. The word "crime" was similar in the island
jargon; everyone knew what the name for "judge" was in
French; and they'd learned enough about the inferno of
red devils from the mouth of Monsieur Lenormand de Mézy's
second wife, a ferocious censor of all concupiscent acts.

Nothing that woman confessed, dressed as she was in a white gown made transparent by the light of the torches, could be the least bit edifying:

> *Minos, juge aux enfers tous les pâles humains.*
> *Ah, combien frémira son ombre épouvantée,*
> *Lorsqu'il verra sa fille à ses yeux présentée,*
> *Contrainte d'avouer tant de forfaits divers,*
> *Et des crimes peut-être inconnus aux enfers!*

Before such immorality, the slaves of the plantation of Lenormand de Mézy insisted on venerating Mackandal. Ti Noël related the Mandingo's tales to his children, teaching them very simple songs he had composed to Mackandal's glory as he combed and groomed the horses. Besides, it was good to remember the One-Armed Man every once in a while, given that he was off in distant lands performing miraculous works and would return on the least expected day.

2

The Great Covenant

Thunder seemed to break in avalanches over the steep inclines of the Morne Rouge, rolling loudly into the far reaches of the gullies when the delegates from all the plantations of the Plaine du Nord arrived in the dense forest of the Bois Cayman, muddied up to their waists and shivering under their wet shirts. To make things worse, the August rain, which went from warm to cold depending on the direction of the wind, had been intensifying since curfew. With his pants sticking to his legs, Ti Noël tried to cover his head with a jute sack folded in the shape of a hood. Despite the darkness, it was certain no spies had slipped into the gathering, which had been announced at the last minute by trustworthy men. Even though they spoke quietly, the whisper of conversations filled the entire forest, blending with the constant drip of rain on the trembling fronds.

Suddenly a powerful voice arose from the middle of the gathering of shadows. A voice with registers that moved without transition from low to high and charged the words with a strange emphasis. That speech filled with anger and screaming was akin to an invocation and a spell. It was Bouckman the Jamaican who spoke that way. Although the thunder erased whole phrases, Ti Noël understood that something had occurred in France, and that some very influential gentlemen had decreed that the blacks should be freed, but that the rich owners of the Cap, who were all monarchist sons-of-bitches, refused to obey. When he got to this point, Bouckman paused and let the rain fall on the trees for several seconds, as if waiting for a stroke of lightning out at sea to begin again. Then, when the rumbling passed, he declared that a pact had been sealed between the elect here and the Great Loas of Africa so that the war could begin under the proper auspices. And from the clamor around him came the final admonition:

"The god of the whites demands crime. Our gods seek vengeance. They will guide our arms and give us aid. Break the image of the god of the whites, who thirsts for our tears, and let us hear inside us the call to freedom!"

The delegates had forgotten the rain that ran from their chins to their bellies, hardening the hide of their belts. A howl rose in the middle of the storm. Next to Bouckman, a bony long-limbed negress was making twirling movements with a ritual machete.

Fai Ogún, Fai Ogún, Fai Ogún, oh!
Damballah m'ap tiré canon,
Fai Ogún, Fai Ogún, Fai Ogún, oh!
Damballah m'ap tiré canon!

Ogun of the Irons, Ogun the Warrior, Ogun of the Forge, Marshal Ogun, Ogun of the Spears, Ogun-Chango, Ogun-Kankanikan, Ogun-Batala, Ogun-Panama, Ogun-Bakule were all invoked now by the priestess of Rada, amid the screaming shadows:

> *Ogún Badagrí*
> *Général sanglant,*
> *Saizi z'orage*
> *Ou scell'orage*
> *Ou fait Kataoun z'eclai!*

The machete suddenly struck the belly of a black pig, which spilled its entrails and lungs after three howls. The delegates were then called by their masters' names, since they had no surnames, and they filed past to have their lips smeared with the pig's foaming blood, which had been collected in a large wooden gourd. After that they all fell headlong on the wet ground. Ti Noël, like the rest, swore he would always obey Bouckman. The Jamaican then embraced Jean-François, Biassou, and Jeannot, who would not be returning to their plantations that night. In this manner he picked the general staff of the revolt. The signal would be given eight days later. There was a very good chance that the Spanish settlers from the other side of the island would lend some aid, as they were mortal enemies of the French. And since it would be necessary to write a proclamation and no one there knew how to write, someone thought of the flexible goose quill pen of the abbot of Haye, the priest of Dondón, a Voltairean who had shown signs of fully supporting the blacks after he had learned about the Declaration of the Rights of Man.

Since the rain had swollen the rivers, Ti Noël had to jump in and swim through the green gully to be in the horse stable before the overseer woke. The dawn bell found him seated and singing up to his waist in a mound of fresh hay, smelling like the sun.

3

The Call of the Conch Shells

Monsieur Lenormand de Mézy was in a terrible mood after his last visit to the Cap. Governor Blanchelande, a monarchist like him, was embittered by the loathsome ramblings of the idiot utopianists in Paris who felt sorry for the fate of black slaves. Oh, it was all too easy to dream about the equality of men while sitting in the Café de la Régence, under the arcades of the Palais Royal, between hands of a game of faro, or else looking at scenes of the ports of the Americas, embellished by wind roses and Tritons with inflated cheeks; at pictures of lazy mulattas and naked washerwomen and siestas under banana trees etched by Abraham Brunias, shown in France amid verses by De Parny. Reading the "Profession of Faith of the Savoyard Vicar," it was very easy to imagine Saint-Domingue as the vegetable paradise of Paul and Virginie, where melons did not hang from tree branches only because they might have fallen from on high and killed a passerby. Already in May, the Constituent Assembly, made up of a liberal, encyclopedist rabble, had agreed to concede political rights to blacks born under manumission. And now, in the shadow of a civil war invoked by the property owners, those ideologues responded in the style of Alexandre-Stanislaus de Wimpffen: "Let the colonies perish rather than a principle."

At around ten o'clock Monsieur Lenormand de Mézy, embittered by his thoughts, went to the outbuildings by the tobacco fields, wanting to force himself on one of the adolescent girls who were at that moment stealing tobacco leaves from the drying barn for their parents to chew. Far away a conch shell had sounded. Surprisingly, the low wail of that conch shell was answered by others in the mountains and jungles. And others, closer to the sea, responded from the farmhouses of Milot. It was as if all the shells of the coast, the Indian seashell horns, the shells used as doorstops, and the shells that lay solitary and petrified on the mountaintops had come together in a choir. Suddenly another conch raised its voice in the main barracks of the plantation. Several high-pitched ones responded from the indigo troughs, the tobacco-drying barn, and the stable. Monsieur Lenormand de Mézy became alarmed and hid behind a bougainvillea bush.

All the doors of the barracks fell at once, torn down from the inside. Armed with stakes, the slaves surrounded the houses of the overseers, taking the tools with them. The accountant, who had appeared in the open with a gun in his hand, was the first to fall, his throat split from top to bottom by a trowel. After smearing their arms with the blood of the white man, the blacks ran toward the main house, screaming death to the owners, the governor, the Good God, and all the Frenchmen of the world. But the majority, driven by long-unsatisfied appetites, rushed into the cellar in search of liquor. Using picks, they split open barrels of pickled fish. With their staves undone, the casks let loose the red wine in spurts, reddening the women's skirts. Grabbed amid screams and shoves, the demijohns of liquor and the carafes of rum broke against the walls. The blacks laughed and fought, sliding on a film of oregano, stewed tomatoes, capers, and herring roe that softened the sound of rancid oil dripping from a rawhide bag. As a joke a naked black man slid into a large container filled with lard. Two old women fought in Congolese over a clay pot. From the ceiling fell hams and slabs of dried fish. Away from the rabble, Ti Noël put his mouth to the spigot of a barrel of Spanish wine and took a long drink, his Adam's apple jerking up and down. Then he went up to the second floor of the main house followed by his oldest sons, eager to rape Mademoiselle Floridor, whose breasts, bulging beneath her flowing robe during her nights of tragedy, were undiminished by the unstoppable passage of time.

4

Dagon Inside the Ark

After hiding for two days in the gloomy bottom of a dry well, Monsieur Lenormand de Mézy, pale with hunger and fear, raised his face slowly over the edge of the parapet. Outside all was silent. The crowds had gone to the Cap, leaving behind columns of smoke rising into the sky, the sources of which became clear when he followed them to the ground. A small munitions dump had just blown up near Le Carrefour des Péres. The master approached the house and passed the accountant's swollen corpse. A terrible stench came from the burned-out dog kennels: there the blacks had paid back an old debt, smearing the doors with tar so that not a single animal would remain alive. Monsieur Lenormand de Mézy entered his room. Mademoiselle Floridor lay spread-eagled on the rug with a sickle stuck in her belly. Her dead hand still held on to one of the legs of the bed with a gesture that was cruelly evocative of one in a silent etching of a sleeping damsel, titled *The Dream*, that adorned the bedroom wall. Monsieur

Lenormand de Mézy broke down in tears and fell next to her. Then he grabbed a rosary and said all the prayers he knew, including one he'd learned as a child for curing chilblains. And thus he spent several days in terror, not daring to leave the house with its doors open to its own ruin, until a messenger on horseback stopped his horse in the backyard so forcefully that the beast slid over the paving stones headlong against a window. The news that the messenger screamed out jarred Monsieur Lenormand de Mézy out of his stupor. The horde had been vanquished. The greenish head of Bouckman the Jamaican, with its mouth ajar, was already filling with worms in the same spot where the flesh of the one-armed Mackandal had been burned to cinders. The total extermination of blacks was being planned, but there still remained armed groups looting the outlying plantations. Without taking the time to give a proper burial to his wife, Monsieur Lenormand de Mézy mounted the messenger's horse, and they galloped wildly down the road to the Cap. In the distance a fusillade went off. The messenger spurred on the horse.

The master arrived just in time to keep Ti Noël and twelve other slaves branded with his iron from being hacked to death in the police station courtyard, where the blacks, tied back-to-back in pairs, awaited their death by machete as a way of preserving gunpowder. Those were the only slaves he had left, and together they were worth at least six thousand Spanish pesos in the Havana market. Monsieur Lenormand de Mézy called for the most extreme physical punishments but asked that the execution be delayed until he had spoken with the governor. Shaking with nervousness, insomnia, and too much coffee, Monsieur Blanchelande paced from one end of his office to the other; it was adorned with a portrait of Louis XVI and Marie Antoinette with the Dauphin. It was difficult to make sense of his scattered monologue, in which his insults against philosophers alternated with references to certain pessimistic passages in letters that he had sent to Paris but were never answered. Anarchy was taking over the world. The colony was going to ruin. The blacks had raped just about every distinguished young lady of the Plaine. After destroying so much lace, finding delight between so many linen bedsheets, and cutting the throats of all those overseers, the blacks could no longer be stopped. Monsieur Blanchelande was in favor of complete and total extermination of the slaves, as well as free blacks and mulattoes. Everyone with African blood in his veins, be he a quadroon, an octoroon, a mameluke, a griffe, or a marabou, should be executed. And one shouldn't be fooled by those shouts of praise coming from slaves when the lights of manger scenes were lit at Christmastime. Père Labat had said it after his first voyage to these islands: blacks behaved like Philistines, adoring Dagon inside the Ark. The governor then pronounced a word that Monsieur Lenormand de Mézy had not paid the least attention to until then: Vodou. Now he remembered that years ago that ruddy and voluminous lawyer from the Cap named Moreau de Saint-Méry had gathered some facts regarding the savage practices of the sorcerers of the mountains, noting that some blacks were snake worshippers. When he remembered this, he was filled with anxiety, realizing that under certain circumstances a drum could mean more than just a goatskin spread tightly over a hollowed-out tree trunk. The slaves had a secret religion that encouraged and united them in their rebellions. They had kept up the practice of this religion under his own nose, perhaps for many years, speaking to one another with those holiday drums without him suspecting anything. How could a cultured person have been concerned about the savage beliefs of people who worshipped snakes?

Deeply depressed by the governor's pessimism, Monsieur Lenormand de Mézy wandered about the streets of the city until nighttime. For a long time he stood before the head of Bouckman, raining insults upon it until he got bored of repeating the same curses. He spent some time in the house of fat Louison, whose girls, wrapped in white muslin, fanned their naked breasts in a courtyard filled with potted malanga plants. But everywhere a foul atmosphere prevailed. Eventually he went to the Street of the Spaniards, hoping to have a drink at the Inn of La Couronne.

Seeing that the inn was closed, he remembered that the cook Henri Christophe had left the business a short time before to wear the uniform of the colonial artillery. Since the golden tin crown, the sign of the restaurant for so many years, had come down, there wasn't a place in the

Cap where one could eat one's fill. Somewhat encouraged by a glass of rum served from a nondescript bar counter or other, Monsieur Lenormand de Mézy started a conversation with the owner of a charcoal sloop, which had been docked for months and which would raise anchor again for Santiago de Cuba as soon as its caulking was finished.

5

Santiago de Cuba

The sloop rounded the cape of the Cap. Back there was the city, forever threatened by the blacks, who were already aware of an offer of military aid from the Spaniards and of the passion with which certain Jacobin humanitarians were beginning to defend their cause. While Ti Noël and his companions were locked in the hold sweating on sacks of charcoal, travelers of a higher class gathered at the stern, taking in the warm breezes of the Windward Passage. There was a female singer of a new company in the Cap, whose café had been burned down the night of the revolt and whose only clothing was a costume from *Dido Abandoned*; an Alsatian musician who had managed to save his clavichord, out of tune on account of the salt air, and who would occasionally interrupt a movement from a sonata by Jean-Frédéric Edelmann to watch a flying fish leap over a bed of yellow clams. A monarchist marquis, two republican officials, a lace maker, and an Italian priest, who was bringing with him his church's monstrance, made up the rest of the ship's passengers.

The night of his arrival in Santiago, Monsieur Lenormand de Mézy went directly to the Tivoli, the thatched-roof theater built recently by the initial French refugees, since the Cuban bodegas with their buzzing flies and their donkeys tied up at the entrance disgusted him. After so much anxiety, so much fear, so many great changes, he found in that café concert a comforting ambience. The best tables were occupied by old friends, plantation owners who, like him, had fled the machetes sharpened with molasses. But the strange thing was that, stripped of their fortune and ruined, with half their families lost and their daughters convalescing from being raped by black men—hardly a small matter—the old settlers, far from mourning, were apparently rejuvenated. Some had the foresight to take their money out of Saint-Domingue and went to New Orleans or else started new coffee plantations in Cuba; those who were unable to salvage anything delighted in the disorder, living from day to day immersed in their lack of obligations, trying to find pleasure in everything. The widower rediscovered the advantages of bachelorhood; the respectable wife gave herself to adultery with the enthusiasm of an inventor; military men enjoyed the lack of reveilles; the Protestant young ladies learned the flattery of the theater, showing themselves off with rouge and beauty marks on their faces. All the bourgeois hierarchies of the colony fell away. What most mattered now was to play the trumpet, embroider a minuet trio with the oboe, or even make the triangle ring in rhythm to the sounds of the Tivoli orchestra. The old notaries copied music and the tax collectors painted twenty Solomonic columns on the large theater curtains. During rehearsals, when all of Santiago took their siestas behind wooden grilles and studded doors, it was not unusual to hear, next to dusty carnival figures from the last Feast of Corpus Christi, a matron previously known for her devotion singing with fainting gestures:

Sous ses lois l'amour veut qu'on jouisse
D'un bonheur qui jamais ne finisse! . . .

Now a great pastoral dance was being advertised—in a style already out of fashion in Paris. The costumes came out of the trunks saved from the pillaging blacks. The dressing rooms made of palm fronds allowed for salacious encounters, while a baritone husband, immersed in his role, was immobilized in a scene by the *aria di bravura* from Monsigny's *Le déserteur.* Passepieds and contredanses were heard for the first time in Santiago de Cuba. The latest wigs, worn by the daughters of the French settlers, twirled to the rhythm of lively minuets already forecasting the waltz. The winds of license, of fantasy, of disorder, blew through the city. Young Creole men began to copy the immigrants' fashions and left the use of outmoded Spanish clothing to the city council members. Some Cuban ladies took classes on French civility behind their confessors' backs and trained themselves in the art of presenting their feet to show off their shoes. At night, when he attended the

Tivoli toward the end of the spectacle after drinking substantial amounts of wine, Monsieur Lenormand de Mézy rose along with the rest to sing, as was the custom established by the refugees, the "Hymn to Saint Louis the King" and the "Marseillaise."

Lazy, unable to put his mind to any idea of a business enterprise, Monsieur Lenormand de Mézy began to divide his time between cards and prayers. He got rid of his slaves, one after the other, to throw his money away in gambling dens, pay his debts at the Tivoli, or take home negresses, of the sort who plied their trade by the port wearing flowers in their hair. At the same time, seeing that the mirror aged him from week to week, he began to fear the imminent call from God. He was a Mason in the old days, but now he distrusted the novelty of those rites. That's why, accompanied by Ti Noël, he would spend long hours moaning and saying short prayers in the cathedral of Santiago. The black man, meanwhile, slept under the portrait of a bishop or listened to the rehearsal of a Christmas carol directed by a dry, loud-mouthed, and very dark old man whom they called Esteban Salas. It was truly impossible to understand why that choirmaster, whom everyone seemed to respect, insisted on having his singers enter the chorus in staggered fashion, the later ones singing what the previous ones had already sung, thus creating a confusion of voices capable of upsetting anyone. But that was, no doubt, pleasing to the sexton, a character to whom Ti Noël attributed great ecclesiastical authority, since he went about armed and wearing pants like a layman. Despite those discordant symphonies, which Don Esteban Salas enriched with bassoons, horns, and boys singing soprano, the black man found in Spanish churches a Vodou warmth he had never found in the Sulpician churches of the Cap. The baroque golds, the human hair of the Christ figures, the heavily ornamented confessionals, the dog of the Dominicans, the dragons crushed by the feet of saints, Saint Anthony's pig, the strange color of Saint Benedict, the black virgins, the figures of Saint George wearing buskins and doublets like actors in French tragedies, and the pastoral musical instruments played during holy days had an engrossing force, a seductive power through symbols, attributes, and signs similar to that which emanated from the *houmfort* altars dedicated to Damballah, the Serpent God. Besides, Santiago was Ogun Fai, the marshal of storms, under whose spell Bouckman's men had risen up. For that reason, Ti Noël, by way of prayer, often recited an old song he had heard from Mackandal:

> *Santiago, I am a child of war:*
> *Santiago,*
> *can't you see I am a child of war?*

6

The Ship of Dogs

One morning the port of Santiago filled with barking. Hundreds of dogs were chained to one another, growling through their muzzles and trying to bite their keepers and one another, throwing themselves at people looking through the bars. Snapping and snapping yet unable to bite, they were led by force of whips into the hold of a sailing ship. And other dogs arrived, and then more, brought by plantation overseers, peasants, and horsemen wearing tall boots. Ti Noël, who had just bought a red snapper under orders from his master, approached the strange vessel into which dogs entered by the dozen and were counted as they passed by a French official who quickly moved the balls of an abacus.

"Where are they taking them?" Ti Noël shouted loudly at a mulatto sailor who was unfolding a net over a hatch.

"To eat blacks!" said the sailor, laughing over the barks.

The answer, given in Kreyol, was a complete revelation for Ti Noël. He ran up the streets toward the cathedral, where other French blacks had gathered, waiting for their masters to finish mass. They were none other than the Dufrené family, who, having lost any hope of keeping their lands, had arrived in Santiago three days earlier after abandoning the plantation made famous by Mackandal's capture. Dufrené's blacks brought important news from the Cap.

From the moment she set sail, Pauline felt a bit like a queen on board that frigate laden with troops going to the Antilles, the rigging groaning to the rhythm of the large waves. Her lover, the actor Lafont, had familiarized her with the roles of a sovereign, reciting for her the most royal verses of *Bajazet* and *Mithridate*. Pauline had a poor memory and yet recalled something about the *Hellespont turning white under our oars*, which rhymed well enough with the wake left behind by *The Ocean*, at full sail with its pennants waving. But now each shift of the wind took with it several alexandrines. After delaying the departure of a whole army so she could satisfy her innocent whim of traveling from Paris to Brest in a litter, she had more important things on her mind. In a lacquered basket she kept handkerchiefs from the island of Mauritius, corselets in a pastoral style, and striped muslin skirts she would wear for the first time on the first hot day, well instructed as she was by the Duchess of Abrantès regarding colonial fashions. On the whole the trip wasn't so boring. The first mass was said from the forecastle by the chaplain once the ship left the bad weather of the Gulf of Gascony, and all the officers gathered in their dress uniforms around General Leclerc, her husband. Some looked splendid, and Pauline, who had good taste in men despite her young age, felt delightfully flattered by the growing desire hidden in all the greetings and attentions directed at her. She knew that when the lamps swung back and forth atop the masts during all those starry nights, hundreds of men dreamed of her in their cabins, castles, and orlops. That's why she was so insistent on feigning that she was meditating every morning on the bow of the frigate next to the forestays, letting her hair loose in the wind and her dress blow tightly against her body, revealing the magnificent shape of her breasts.

A few days after passing through the Azores Channel, Pauline gazed at the white Portuguese chapels of the villages in the distance and discovered that the sea was changing. Now it was adorned with bunches of yellow grapes floating eastward; it brought forth needlefish that seemed made of green glass; jellyfish like blue bladders pulling long red filaments; toothy fish that looked threatening; and squid that appeared to become tangled in barely visible brides' veils. They had now entered heat so fierce it made the brilliant officers unbutton their vests; Leclerc allowed them to go about bare chested with their jackets open. During a particularly suffocating night, Pauline abandoned her cabin dressed only in her nightgown and went to lie down on the quarterdeck, which had been reserved so she could take her long naps. The sea was green and strangely phosphorescent. A faint breeze seemed to descend from the stars, which grew more numerous with each day's run. At dawn the sentry was happily disconcerted by discovering the presence of a nude woman asleep on a folded sail, under the shade of the mizzen jib. Believing she was one of the maids, he almost sneaked up on her. But a movement of the sleeping beauty announcing she was about to wake made him realize that before him lay the body of Pauline Bonaparte. She rubbed her eyes and smiled like a child. Still chilly from the morning breeze, believing she was hidden from view by the sails, she emptied several buckets of water over her shoulders. From that night on she always slept in the open air, and her generous carelessness became well-known to so many that even the dry Monsieur d'Esmenard, who would be in charge of organizing the repressive police of Saint-Domingue, came to daydream before his students, evoking in her honor the Greek statue of Galatea.

The sight of the City of the Cap and the Plaine du Nord, with the mountains in the background blurred by the mist rising from the sugarcane fields, charmed Pauline. She had read about the loves of Paul and Virginie and knew a pretty Creole contredanse, of unusual rhythm, titled "The Island Girl," published in Paris in the rue du Saumon. Feeling somewhat like a bird of paradise and somewhat like a lyrebird in her muslin skirts, she discovered the finery of young ferns, the brown juice of the loquat, and large leaves that could be folded up like a fan. At night

Leclerc spoke to her, complaining about slave rebellions, the difficulties with monarchist settlers, and threats of all sorts. Foreseeing great dangers, he had purchased a house on Île de la Tortue. But Pauline didn't pay much attention. She was engrossed in *The Negro Equaled by Few Whites*, the lachrymose novel by Joseph Lavallée, and happily enjoying the luxury and abundance she had never known in her childhood, filled as it had been with dry figs, goat cheese, and rancid olives. She lived not far from the main church in a huge house of white stone surrounded by a shady garden. She had a blue mosaic swimming pool built under the cover of tamarind trees in which she swam naked. At first she had her French maids give her massages, but one day it occurred to her that the hands of a man would be more vigorous and strong, and she hired Soliman, a longtime steward of a bathhouse, who, besides caring for her body, rubbed her with almond cream, removed unwanted hair, and polished her toenails. Whenever she had him bathe her, Pauline felt a mischievous pleasure in rubbing against his strong flanks under the water. She knew the servant was constantly tormented by desire and looked at her sideways with the false meekness of a dog that's been beaten too much. She would hit him softly with a green branch, laughing as he pretended to be hurt. In truth, she was grateful for the solicitous way he paid attention to her beauty. Sometimes she allowed the black man, as recompense for an errand quickly run or a well-made communion, to kiss her legs while he knelt before her on the ground with a gesture that Bernardin de Saint-Pierre would have interpreted as a symbol of the noble gratitude of a simple soul before the generous ideals of the Enlightenment.

In this fashion time passed between sleeping and waking, and she believed herself a little bit like Virginie, a little bit like Atala, despite the fact that at times, when Leclerc traveled to the south, she amused herself with the youthful ardor of a handsome officer. But one afternoon, the French hairdresser who did her hair aided by four black workers fell in front of her vomiting dark, half-clotted blood. Dressed in a silver-mottled bodice, a horrible killjoy had begun to buzz in Pauline Bonaparte's tropical dream.

7

Saint Calamity

Urged on by Leclerc, who had just gone through towns devastated by the epidemic, Pauline fled the following morning to La Tortue in the company of Soliman and the maids, loaded down with bundles. Initially she distracted herself by bathing in a sandy cove and leafing through the memoirs of the surgeon Alexandre Olivier Exquemelin, who knew so well the habits and misdeeds of the corsairs and buccaneers of the Americas. The only evidence of their life on the island was the ruins of an ugly fortress. She laughed when the mirror in her room revealed to her that her skin, browned by the sun, had turned her into a splendid mulatta. But the respite was short-lived. One afternoon Leclerc disembarked on La Tortue with his body riven by a sinister shivering. His eyes were yellow. The military doctor who accompanied him had him take strong doses of rhubarb.

Pauline was horrified. Faded images of a cholera epidemic she had witnessed in Ajaccio came to her mind. The coffins left the houses on the shoulders of men in black; the widows veiled in black howled at the foot of the fig trees; the daughters also dressed in black wanted to throw themselves into the graves of their fathers and had to be pulled forcibly out of the cemetery. Suddenly she felt great anxiety caused by the same feelings of being shut in she had experienced many times as a child. In those moments La Tortue, with its parched soil, its red cliffs, its wastelands of cacti and cicadas, its always visible sea, resembled her native island. There was no escape. Behind the door a man wheezed gravely, showing a total lack of consideration in bringing death to her under his uniform. Convinced that the doctors were useless, Pauline listened to the advice of Soliman, who recommended burning incense, indigo, and lemon peels, as well as offering orations of extraordinary power to the Great Judge, Saint George, and Saint Calamity. She allowed the doors of the house to be washed with aromatic plants and discarded tobacco. She knelt at the foot of a crucifix of dark wood, reciting a flamboyant, somewhat primitive devotional litany, screaming along with the black man at the end of each prayer, *Malo, Presto, Pasto, Effacio, Amèn.* Besides, those incantations, along with hammering nails in the form of a cross to the trunk of a lemon tree, shook awake in her the lees of her Corsican blood, which were closer to the living cosmogony of the black man than the lies of the Directory, whose lack of faith she had come to accept. Now she repented of having mocked so often matters of holiness simply to follow the day's fashions.

Leclerc's agony increased her fear and led her to the world of powers that Soliman invoked with his spells. He was the true lord of the island, the only possible defender against the blows of the other shore, the only possible doctor before the uselessness of the medical manuals. To keep the evil airs from crossing the water, the black man set little boats on the waves, made from coconut halves, all of them decorated with ribbons taken from Pauline's sewing kit. They were additional tributes to Aguassu, Lord of the Sea. One morning Pauline discovered the model of a battleship among Leclerc's things. She ran to the beach and gave it to Soliman so that he could add the work of art to his offerings. They had to defend themselves from the sickness in any way possible: promises, penance, hair shirts, fasting, invocations to whoever was listening, even though at times the False Enemy of her childhood raised his hairy ear. Suddenly Pauline began wandering strangely about the house, avoiding stepping on the intersections of the tiles, which were cut squarely—this was a well-known fact—by the impious insistence of the Freemasons, who wanted people to step on the cross every hour of the day. Rather than essential oils and fresh mint water, Soliman now spilled ointments made from rum, crushed seeds, oily juices, and the blood of birds on her chest. One morning the French maids discovered with horror that the black man was doing a strange dance around Pauline, who was kneeling on the floor with her hair loose. Wearing nothing but a belt from which hung a white handkerchief by way of a loincloth,

Soliman jumped like a bird, waving a rusty machete. Both let out long wails that came from deep in the chest and sounded like the howls of dogs at full moon. A rooster with its throat cut flopped around on a bed of corn kernels. When he realized that one of the female slaves was watching the scene, the black man kicked the door shut in a fit of rage. That afternoon various images of the saints appeared hanging upside down from the roof beams. Soliman never left Pauline's side now, sleeping on a red rug in her bedroom.

The death of Leclerc in a fit of black vomit led Pauline to the edge of madness. Now the tropics and its patient vultures perched on the roofs of houses where people sweated through their agony became abominable to her. After dressing her husband in his full-dress uniform and placing his body in a cedar coffin, Pauline quickly boarded the *Swift-sure*. She was thin and haggard and her chest was covered with scapulars. But soon the wind from the east rose up, bringing the sensation that Paris grew ever closer before the prow, and the salt air that was gnawing on the metal rings of the coffin began to release the young widow from her suffering. One afternoon when the choppy sea made the timbers of the keel moan violently, her mourning veil got caught in the spurs of a young officer who had been charged with honoring and guarding the remains of General Leclerc. In the basket containing her shabby Creole costumes was also an amulet to Papa Legba made by Soliman, destined to open for Pauline Bonaparte all the roads that led to Rome.

Pauline's parting signaled the end of good sense in the colony. Under the rule of Rochambeau, the last owners of the Plaine lost all hope of returning to the comforts of old and gave themselves to a vast orgy without limits or truce. Nobody paid attention to the clocks, nor did the nights end at sunup. The wine had to be exhausted, meat eaten, and pleasure satisfied before a catastrophe might put an end to the pleasure. The governor dispensed favors for women. The ladies of the Cap mocked dead Leclerc's edict that "white women who prostituted themselves with blacks be returned to France, whatever their rank." Many females gave themselves over to tribadism, appearing in dances with mulattas whom they called their cocottes. The daughters of slaves were forced into sex while still children. Down that road things devolved into horror. On feast days Rochambeau had his dogs devour blacks, and when they hesitated in attacking humans in the presence of so many brilliant people dressed in silk, a victim was wounded with a sword and blood drawn to incite the dogs. Figuring such acts would intimidate the blacks, the governor ordered hundreds of mastiffs be brought from Cuba.

"On leur fera bouffer du noir!"

The day the ship seen by Ti Noël entered the port of the Cap, it came together with another sailboat coming from Martinique loaded with poisonous snakes the general wanted to let loose in the Plaine that they might attack the peasants who lived in isolated shacks and aided escaped slaves hiding in the mountains. But those serpents, creatures of Damballah, were to die without laying eggs, disappearing as completely as the last settlers from the ancien régime. Now the Great Loas favored the weapons of the blacks. Those who invoked the warrior gods were the ones winning the battles. Ogun Badagri guided the charges of the cold weapons against the last trenches of the goddess Reason. And, as in all combats worthy of being remembered because someone stopped the sun or tore down walls with a trumpet, there were in those days men who blocked the mouths of enemy cannons with their chests and men who had the power to deflect the lead of rifles from their bodies. It was then that some black priests, who hadn't been tonsured or ordained, appeared in the fields. They were called the Fathers of the Savannah, and they were as knowledgeable in the act of reciting Latin over the straw mattress of a dying man as the French priests. But they were better understood, because when they recited the Our Father or the Hail Mary they knew how to inject the text with certain accents and inflections that were similar to those of hymns everyone knew. Finally, certain matters of the living and the dead were starting to be taken care of within the family.

PART THREE

Everywhere there were royal crowns made of gold, some so heavy they could hardly be lifted from the floor.

—Karl Ritter, witness to the looting of Sans-Souci

1

The Signs

An old black man, still strong on his gnarled and scaly feet, left the schooner newly docked on the wharf of Saint-Marc. Far away to the north, a crest of mountains colored a slightly darker blue than the sky's drew a familiar scene. Without further delay, Ti Noël grabbed a heavy stick made of lignum vitae and left the city. A long time had passed since a landowner from Santiago won him in an all-or-nothing game of *mus* from Monsieur Lenormand de Mézy, who died soon after in abject poverty. Under the hand of his Cuban master he had lived a much easier life than that imposed by the French slave owners of the Plaine du Nord. And so, saving the coins his master gave him yearly as a Christmas bonus, he'd managed to pay the sum demanded by the owner of a fishing boat to travel on deck. Even though he was marked by two irons, Ti Noël was a free man. He was now walking on a land where slavery had been abolished forever.

On the first day of his march he reached the banks of

the Artibonite and sat down under cover of a tree to spend the night. At dawn he started walking again, following a road that stretched between wild vines and bamboo. The men washing their horses screamed things he hardly understood, but he answered in his way, saying whatever came into his mind. Besides, Ti Noël had never been alone even though he was alone. A long time ago he had acquired the art of conversing with chairs and pots, or else with a cow, a guitar, or his own shadow.

Here the people were happy. But farther on, at a turn of the trail, the plants and the trees seemed to have dried up, turning into skeletons on an earth that had gone from red and lumpy to something resembling cellar dust. There were no longer any light-filled cemeteries made up of small white plaster graves the size of doghouses. Here the dead were buried by the side of the road in a silent, hostile plain overgrown with cacti and myrrh trees. Sometimes an abandoned blanket, still draped over four wooden posts, meant the sudden flight of its inhabitants from malevolent miasmas. All the vegetation had sharp edges, darts, thorns, and harmful excretions. The few men Ti Noël ran into did not respond to his greeting, passing by with their eyes fixed on the ground like the snouts of their dogs. Suddenly the black man stopped, breathing deeply. A sacrificed goat hung from a thorn-covered tree. The ground was filled with warnings: three stones in a semicircle and a small branch broken in the shape of a pointed arch by way of an entrance. Farther on, several black chickens tied by one leg swung head down from a greasy branch. Finally, at the end of the signs, a particularly evil-looking tree stood, its trunk covered with black thorns, surrounded by offerings. Among its roots someone had placed several gnarled and twisted crutches belonging to Legba, the Lord of the Roads.

Ti Noël fell on his knees and gave thanks to heaven for having provided him the joy of returning to the land of the Great Pacts. Because he knew—as did all the French blacks of Santiago de Cuba—that Dessalines's triumph was due to extensive preparations, in which Loco, Petro, Ogun Ferraille, Brise-Pimba, Caplaou-Pimba, Marinette Bois-Cheche, and all the divinities of gunpowder and fire had intervened in a series of possessions of such violence that some men had been hurled into the air or thrown to the ground by the incantations. Afterward, blood, gunpowder, flour, and coffee grounds were mixed to create the leavening capable of turning the ancestors' heads, while the consecrated drums beat and the irons of the initiates crossed over a fire. At the height of the exaltation, a possessed man had mounted the backs of two whinnying men and they were joined together in the profile of a stamping centaur, descending in a horse's gallop beyond the night, beyond many nights, toward the sea that licked the shores of the world of the Great Powers.

2

Sans-Souci

After several days of walking, Ti Noël began to recognize certain places. From the taste of the water, he learned he had bathed there many times, but farther down, in the stream that snaked toward the coast. He passed by the cave where Mackandal had once macerated his poisonous plants. Growing impatient, he descended through the narrow valley of Dondón until he came to the Plaine du Nord. Then, following the coast, he walked toward Lenormand de Mézy's old plantation.

He knew he'd arrived when he saw the three ceibas planted in a triangle. But nothing remained: not the indigo room or the dryers or the stables or the meat-curing rooms. All that stood of the house was a brick chimney covered with ivy, which was now half dead from too much sun and not enough shade; of the warehouses, some tiles stuck in mud; of the chapel, the iron rooster weathervane. Here and there rose pieces of wall that seemed like thick broken letters. The pines, the grapevines, and the European trees had all disappeared, as had the vegetable garden

where asparagus had once whitened and the hearts of arti-
chokes thickened among sprigs of mint and marjoram. The
whole plantation had turned into a wasteland crossed by a
road. Ti Noël sat on one of the cornerstones of the old mansion, now a stone like any other stone for those who had no
memory of the place. He was talking to the ants when an
unexpected noise made him turn his head. Coming toward
him at a full gallop were several riders in resplendent uniforms with blue dolmans covered in sashes and other trap-
pings, ornamental collars, tasseled braids, and suede pants
trimmed with galloons. On their heads they wore shakos
crested with blue plumes and on their legs hussar-style
boots. Accustomed to the simple colonial uniforms worn by
Spaniards, Ti Noël was surprised by the pomp of a Napoleonic style that men of his race had taken to a degree never
imagined by the Corsican's generals. The officers passed by
him as if surrounded by a cloud of gold dust heading toward
Milot. Intrigued, the old man followed the horses along the
dirt road.

Leaving a copse, he had the sensation of entering a
sumptuous orchard. All the land surrounding the town of
Milot was divided into carefully tended plots, vegetable gardens squared off by irrigation ditches, the ridges between
furrows greening with tender shoots. Many people were
working in those fields under the watch of soldiers armed
with whips, who, on occasion, threw a pebble in the direction of a slacker. "Prisoners," Ti Noël thought, seeing that
the guards were black and the workers as well, which con-
tradicted certain notions he had acquired in Santiago de

Cuba on the nights he was allowed to attend the dance parties of French blacks. But now the old man had stopped, marveling at the most unexpected and imposing spectacle he had seen in his long life. On a background of mountains ribbed purple by deep grooves rose a pink palace with arched windows, made as if to float on a base of tall stairs. To one side were long tiled structures, probably the living quarters, the military barracks, and the horse stables. On the other side was a round building crowned by a cupola resting on white columns, out of which several priests wearing surplices were walking. As he came closer Ti Noël saw terraces, statues, arcades, gardens, pergolas, artificial streams, and boxwood labyrinths. At the foot of massive pilasters that held up a huge sun made of black wood, two bronze lions stood guard. On the marching ground, a bustle of officers dressed in white and young captains wearing bicorns came and went shining brilliantly, their sabers making slapping sounds on their thighs. Through an open window he could see and hear a dance orchestra in rehearsal. Ladies leaned out of the palace windows, their heads crowned with feathers and their breasts pushed up by the high waist of the dresses then in fashion. In the patio two liveried coachmen were washing an enormous gilded carriage, totally covered in bas-relief suns. As he passed in front of the circular building that the priests had left, Ti Noël realized it was a church, filled with curtains, tapestries, and canopies that covered a tall image of the Immaculate Conception.

But what surprised Ti Noël the most was the discovery that this marvelous world was a world of blacks such as the French governors had never known. Black were those beautiful ladies, with firm behinds, who were now dancing the rondeau around a fountain of Tritons; black were those ministers in white stockings who descended the grand stairs with sheepskin purses under their arms; black was the cook with an ermine tail on his cap, who received a deer from the shoulders of several villagers led by the Chief Huntsman; black those hussars who trotted around in the riding pen; black the Head Butler, with a silver chain hanging around his neck, who, in the company of the Principal Master of Falconry, observed the rehearsals of black actors in an outdoor theater; black those white-wigged footmen whose gilded buttons were counted by a majordomo wearing a green jacket; lastly, black, oh so very black, was the Immaculate Conception, who loomed over the main altar of the chapel, smiling sweetly toward the black musicians rehearsing a Hail Mary. Ti Noël realized he was in Sans-Souci, the favorite residence of King Henri Christophe, who had once been the chef on the Street of the Spaniards and the owner of the Inn of La Couronne, and who today had coins minted with his initials over the proud emblem *God, my cause and my sword.*

The old man suddenly received a tremendous blow on his shoulder. Before he could complain, a guard was kicking him and forcing him toward one of the barracks. Seeing himself shut in a jail cell, Ti Noël yelled out that he knew Henri Christophe personally, and he also knew that he had married Marie-Louise Coidavid, the niece of a freed lace maker who often went to the plantation of Lenormand de Mézy. But no one paid any attention. In the afternoon he was taken along with other prisoners to the foot of the Bonnet à l'Évêque, where there were large mounds of construction materials. They handed him a brick.

"Take it up there. And come back for another!"

"I am very old."

Ti Noël received a blow to the head. Without further objection, he began the steep ascent of the mountain, joining in a long line of children, pregnant girls, women, and old people, who were also carrying bricks. The old man turned his head toward Milot. In the afternoon the palace glowed more intensely pink than before. Next to a bust of Pauline Bonaparte that had once adorned her house in the Cap, the little princesses Athénaïs and Améthyste, dressed in satin with braided trimmings, were playing badminton. A little farther away the queen's chaplain—the only light-skinned person in the group—was reading Plutarch's *Parallel Lives* to the crown prince, under the satisfied look of Henri Christophe, who strolled through the queen's gardens followed by his ministers. As he passed, His Majesty distractedly grabbed a white rose, newly open by a topiary shaped like a crown and phoenix at the foot of the marble allegories.

3

The Sacrifice of the Bulls

Atop the Bonnet à l'Évêque rose that second mountain thorny with scaffolding, the Citadelle of La Ferrière. A large growth of red fungi, smooth and obstinate like brocade, crept up the sides of the main tower, having already covered the fortifications at the base, spreading its polyps over the ocher-colored walls. On that mass of fired bricks the Citadelle rose past the clouds in such a way that its perspectives defied the limits of one's sight. From its shadows opened tunnels, hallways, secret pathways, and chimneys. An aquarium light, glaucous and dyed a greenish color by ferns that grew thickly over the void, descended like a veil of mist from the heights of the embrasures and vents. The stairways to hell connected three principal batteries with the powder magazine, the artillerymen's chapel, the kitchens, the cisterns, the foundry, and the dungeons. In the middle of the parade ground, a number of bulls had their throats slit daily to mix the blood into a mortar that would make the fortress invulnerable. On the side facing the sea, which dominated the immense panorama of the Plaine, workers were already plastering the living areas of the Royal Palace, the women's rooms, the dining halls, and the billiard rooms. Suspension bridges were built on wagon wheel axles affixed to the walls to carry brick and stone to the highest terraces. They hung between chasms on either side, making the workers' stomachs queasy. Often a black man disappeared into the void, taking with him a load of mortar. Someone else took his place and no one gave any further thought to the fallen one. Hundreds of men worked in the innards of the huge construction site, always under the threat of the whip and the rifle, completing works that were never before envisioned, except in the architecture imagined by Piranesi. Raised by ropes over the mountain's escarpments came the first cannons, which were placed on cedar carriages one after the other in domed hallways forever in gloom. Those cannons controlled all the passes and gorges of the countryside. There was Scipio and Hannibal and Hamilcar, made of smoothly polished, almost gilded bronze, next to those born after '89, with the still-uncertain insignia stating *Liberty, Equality*. There was a Spanish cannon on whose back one could read the melancholy inscription *Faithful but Unfortunate*, and others, with wider mouths and more fancily adorned backs bearing the Sun King's insolent emblem, *Ultima Ratio Regum*.

When Ti Noël finally put down his brick at the foot of a wall, it was near midnight. Nevertheless, the construction work continued by the light of bonfires and torches. On the roads men fell asleep on huge blocks of stone, atop loose cannons, next to mules with knees scabbed from so many falls on the way up. Exhausted, the old man dropped to the side of a moat under a drawbridge. At dawn he was awakened by a whiplash. Up above, the sacrificial bulls bellowed. New scaffolding rose to the cold clouds, as the whole mountain was covered in neighs, screams, trumpet calls, the crack of whips, and the squeal of ropes that had swollen with dew. Ti Noël began to descend to Milot in search of another brick. Along the way he could see that on the flanks of the mountain, on every trail and shortcut, were single lines packed with women, children, and old people all carrying the same bricks to leave them at the foot of the fortress, which was being erected like a termite mound or an anthill using those grains of fired clay that rose toward it without pause, in sun and in rain, from feast day to feast day. Soon Ti Noël learned that the process had lasted more than twelve years and that the whole population of the north had been mobilized by force to work on that astonishing construction site. All attempts to protest had been silenced in blood. Moving, always moving, up and down and down and up, the black man began to think that the chamber orchestras of Sans-Souci, the fancy uniforms, and the statues of white nudes warming in the sun on their ornamental bases amid the boxwood hedges of the flower beds were the result of a slavery as abominable as the one he had known in the plantation owned by Monsieur Lenormand de Mézy. Worse still, since it was an infinitely miserable thing to be beaten up by a black man as dark as oneself, as thick-lipped and nappy-haired, as flat-nosed as oneself; as equal, as low-born, as marked by iron, possibly, as oneself. It was as if in the same household the children hit the parents, the grand-child hit the grandmother, and the daughters-in-law hit the mother at the stove. Besides, in past times, the settlers were very careful about killing one of their slaves, unless by accident, because killing a slave was to open a great hole in one's pocket, while here the death of a black man cost nothing to the public treasury; having an abundance of child-bearing negresses would forever guarantee a steady stream of laborers to carry bricks to the top of the Bonnet à l'Évêque.

King Christophe often went to the Citadelle on horseback accompanied by his officers in order to check on the progress of the construction. Short, very strong, and barrel-chested, with a Roman nose and a beard partly hidden by the embroidered collar of his dress coat, the monarch inspected the batteries, forges, and workshops, his spurs clinking as he ascended the interminable stairs. His Napoleonic bicorn sported a bicolored cockade. At times, with a simple gesture of his riding crop, he ordered the death of a lazy man surprised in the act of relaxing, or the execution of peasants who were taking their time moving a block of stone along a steep incline. And he always wound up sitting on a chair brought to the highest terrace overlooking the sea, at the edge of an abyss that made even the most hardened men close their eyes. Then, without any worries or concerns weighing on him, sitting above everything, including his own shadow, he measured the full extent of his power. In case France might decide to reconquer the island, he, Henri Christophe, *God, my cause and my sword*, could resist there above the clouds, as many years as might be necessary, with his court, his army, his chaplains, his musicians, his African pages, and his buffoons. Fifteen thousand men would live with him inside those Cyclopean walls without lacking anything. With the drawbridge of the main gate up, the Citadelle of La Ferrière would become the country itself, with its independence, its monarch, its living quarters, and its pomp and splendor. Because below, forgetting the suffering caused by its construction, the blacks of the Plaine would raise their eyes toward the fortress, filled with corn, gunpowder, iron, and gold, thinking that there, above the birds, while life below would sound remotely of bells and cock crows, a king of their own race awaited close to the sky, which is the same everywhere, the thundering bronze hooves of Ogun's ten thousand horses. It was for a reason that those towers had been erected over the loud bellowing of bulls with their throats slit open, their testicles exposed to the sun, by builders fully aware of the profound significance of the sacrifice, even though they might tell the ignorant rabble that it was simply an advanced technique of military masonry.

4

Walled In

When the works of the Citadelle were near completion and craftsmen became more important for the work than the brick bearers, discipline lessened, and even though mortars and culverins were still being carried up the steep mountain cliffs, many women were able to return to their pots, which were now covered with spiderwebs. Among those who were let go one morning was Ti Noël, who scurried out without turning to look at the fortress, now clear of scaffolding on the side of the battery of the Royal Princesses. The tree trunks that were being rolled upward by means of levers would be used for building the floors of the living quarters. But none of this interested Ti Noël any longer. His only goal was to settle down on the old lands of Lenormand de Mézy, like an eel returning to the mud where it was born.

Once back on the property he felt a sense of ownership of that soil, the topography of which had meaning only for him, and he began to clear the overgrowth away from the ruins. Two felled trees uncovered a piece of wall. The blue tiles of the dining room appeared from under the leaves of a wild calabash patch. He used palm fronds to cover the chimney of the old kitchen, only half of which remained standing, and thus he made a space he could crawl into. He spread the ground with sprigs of hay on which he could lie to rest from the blows he'd received along the trails of the Bonnet à l'Évêque.

In that manner he survived the winds of the winter and the rains that followed, and he came to summer with his belly swollen from eating too much unripe fruit and watery mangoes, not daring to show himself on the roads for fear of running across Christophe's people, who were looking for men to build a new palace, perhaps the very one, rumor had it, that would rise over the banks of the Artibonite River with as many windows as the year had days. Several months passed without incident and Ti Noël, tired of being miserable, made a trip to the city of the Cap, never straying too far from the sea on that same path, now almost completely covered over, that he had taken following his master on their way back to the plantation riding a half-broken horse, of the sort that trot along making a sound like rubbed cordovan leather and still have on their necks the wrinkles of a colt. The city is good. In the city a crooked hand always finds things to stuff into a sack slung over the shoulder. In the city there are always good-hearted prostitutes who give alms to old men; there are markets with some type of music, tamed animals, talking dolls, and cooks who appreciate someone who, instead of mentioning hunger, points instead to the liquor bottle. Ti Noël felt a great cold snaking into his bones, and he longed for those bottles of old—the ones in the basement of the plantation house—square, made with thick crystal and filled with rinds, grasses, berries, and watercress steeped in alcohol that gave off soft, calming odors.

Ti Noël found an entire city waiting for death. It was as if all the windows and doors of the houses, all the jalousies and portholes had turned toward the one corner of the Archbishopric, with an intensity of expectation that deformed the façades into grimaces. The roofs stretched their eaves, the corners sharpened to an edge, and the humidity drew ears on the walls. On the corner of the Archbishopric a rectangle of cement had just dried in the wall, except for an air vent left open. From that hole, black as a toothless mouth, came forth wails so horrible they made the people shiver and children weep inside their houses. Whenever this happened, pregnant women would bring their hands to their bellies and some passersby would break into a run and cross themselves. And the wails continued, all that senseless screaming at the corner of the Archbishopric until the throat, bleeding now, would fall into anathemas, dark threats, prophecies, and curses. Weeping followed from deep in the chest, with childlike whimpers in the voice of an old man, worse than the wailing of before. Finally the tears broke into a rhythmic snorting that would die down in a long, asthmatic cadence until it became mere breathing. These sounds were repeated day and night at the corner of the Archbishopric. No one slept in the Cap. No one dared walk on the surrounding streets. Inside the houses people whispered their prayers in the rooms farthest from the street. No one had the courage, even, to make mention of what was happening because the Capuchin who'd been immured inside the Archbishopric, buried alive in his chapel, was none other than Corneille Breille, the Duke of Anse, confessor of Henri Christophe. He'd been condemned to die there, at the foot of a newly repaired wall, for wanting to leave for France knowing all of the king's secrets and all of the secrets of the Citadelle, whose red towers had already been struck by lightning several times. Queen Marie-Louise implored her husband in vain, embracing his boots. Henri Christophe, who had just insulted Saint Peter for sending a new storm over his fortress, was not going to be scared by the useless excommunication of a French Capuchin. Besides, to dispel any doubt, Sans-Souci had a new favorite: a Spanish chaplain with a large shovel hat, as much of a busybody as he was a gossip, given to singing the mass in a beautiful bass voice. Everyone called him Juan de Dios. Tired of the chickpeas and the dry meat eaten by the gruff Spaniards on the other side of the island, the wily friar found great pleasure in the Haitian court, whose ladies overwhelmed him with shiny fruit and Portuguese wines. It was rumored that some of his comments, spoken offhandedly in the presence of Henri Christophe while he taught his greyhounds to jump in honor of the king of France, were the cause of the terrible demise of Corneille Breille.

After a week of being immured, the Capuchin's voice was almost imperceptible, dying in a last sigh, imagined rather than heard. And then silence came to the corner of the Archbishopric. The long silence of a city that had ceased to believe in silence, broken only by the ignorant squeal of a newborn, finally ended, and life resumed its usual bustle, with the calls of street vendors, chatter, small talk, and songs to hang clothes by. It was then that Ti Noël was able to throw some things in his sack, getting a few coins from a drunk sailor that allowed him to drink five glasses in a row. Weaving drunkenly under the light of the moon, he took the way back, vaguely remembering a song from earlier times that he would always sing when returning from the city, a song that was loaded with insults to a king. That was the important thing: *to a king*. And so, as he tired of insulting Henri Christophe, his crown, and his progeny, he found the walk so easy and quick that, when he threw himself on the mat of hay, he asked himself if he had truly gone to the Cap.

5

Chronicle of August Fifteenth

Quasi palma exaltata sum in Cades, et quasi plantatio rosae in Jericho. Quasi oliva speciosa in campis, et quasi platanus exaltata sum juxta aquam in plateis. Sicut cinnamonum et balsamum aromatizans odorem dedi: quasi myrrah electa dedi suavitatem odoris.

Without understanding the Latin that Juan de Dios González intoned in his most effective baritone, Queen Marie-Louise found that morning a perfect harmony among the odor of the incense, the fragrance of orange blossoms emanating from a nearby patio, and certain words from the liturgical lesson of the day that alluded to the names of perfumes listed on the porcelain jars of the apothecary of Sans-Souci. Henri Christophe, on the other hand, couldn't follow the mass with the necessary attention, since his chest was tightening with inexplicable misgivings. Against everyone's wishes he had wanted the Mass of the Assumption to be sung in the church of Limonade. Its veined gray marble gave a delightful impression of coolness, allowing him to sweat less under the jacket buckles and the weight of his decorations. Nevertheless, the king felt himself surrounded by hostile forces. The people, who had acclaimed him on his arrival, were full of bad intentions on remembering too vividly the harvests of a fertile soil that were lost as a result of having the men work on the construction of the Citadelle. In some far-off house, he suspected, someone would be sticking his image with pins or hanging it by the neck with a knife in his heart. In the distance he could hear at times the beating of drums that most probably didn't play in supplication for his long life. But now the Offertory was beginning.

Assumpta est Maria in caelum; gaudent Angeli, collaudantes benedicunt Dominum, alleluia!

Suddenly Juan de Dios González began to retreat toward the royal seats, tripping clumsily on the three marble steps. The queen dropped her rosary. The king grabbed the handle of his sword. Before the altar, facing the faithful, another priest stood, as if born out of the air, his shoulders and arms drooping awkwardly. While the figure gradually acquired firmness and shape, a frightening voice came from his lipless, toothless mouth, black as a bull's eye, which filled the nave with the vibrations of an organ at full register and made the lead of the stained glass windows tremble.

Absolve, Domine, animas omnium fidelium defunctorum ab omni vinculo delictorum . . .

The name Corneille Breille crossed Christophe's mind, leaving him speechless. For the figure was none other than the immured archbishop, whose death and decay everyone knew, there in the middle of the main altar, dressed in ecclesiastical pomp and crying out the Dies Irae. When the cymbals rolled and the words *Coget omnes ante thronum* sounded, Juan de Dios González collapsed, moaning before the queen's feet. Confused, Henri Christophe stood still until the *Rex tremendae majestatis.* At that moment a bolt of lightning struck the church tower with a deafening boom, cracking all the bells at once. The precentors, the thuribles, the lectern, and the pulpit came down. The king lay on the floor, paralyzed, with his eyes fixed on the ceiling beams. But now the specter gave a great leap and sat on one of those beams, in the exact spot where Christophe might see him, spreading his arms and legs to make his brocade appear larger and filthier. In his ears Christophe heard a beating which could be that of his own veins or that of the drums pounding in the mountains. Taken out of the church in the arms of his officers, the king mumbled some vague curses, threatening with death all the people of Limonade if the cocks crowed. While he was cared for by Marie-Louise and the princesses, the peasants, terrified by the monarch's ravings, began to lower their hens and roosters hidden in baskets into the darkness of the deepest wells so that they might forget about clucking and crowing. Donkeys were driven away into the mountains. The horses were muzzled so that their neighing might not be misinterpreted.

And that afternoon, the heavy royal carriage entered

the parade ground of Sans-Souci, its six horses at a gallop. With his shirt open, the king was taken to his rooms. He fell into bed like a sack of chains. More cornea than iris, his eyes expressed a furor that came from the deepest parts of him because he couldn't move his arms or legs. The doctors began to rub his inert body with a mixture of rum, gunpowder, and red pepper. Everywhere in the palace the medicines, tisanes, salts, and unguents saturated the tepid salons, filled to capacity with functionaries and courtesans. The princesses Athénaïs and Améthyste wept against the breast of their American governess. The queen, little worried about etiquette in those moments, crouched in a corner of the anteroom and watched over a boiling brew of roots she was heating on a charcoal burner. The glow of its flame added a strange realism to the colors of a Gobelin tapestry that hung on the wall showing Venus in Vulcan's forge. Her Majesty asked for a fan to liven the slow fire. An evil atmosphere surrounded the dusky shadows who were all too eager to hold on to material things. No one could tell for sure if drums were beating in the mountains, but, at times, a rhythm descending from the high distances blended strangely with the Hail Mary of the women praying in the Throne Room, resonating sympathetically in more than one unconfessed breast.

6

Ultima Ratio Regum

The following Sunday, as the sun set, Henri Christophe had the impression that his numb knees and arms would respond to a great effort of will. Turning this way and that to get out of bed, he let his feet fall on the floor, remaining twisted with his back sideways on the bed. His footman Soliman helped him straighten up. Then the king was able to walk to the window with measured steps, like a great automaton. The servant called the queen and princesses, and they entered the room quietly, moving to a dark corner under an equestrian portrait of His Majesty. They knew that the people in Haut-le-Cap were drinking to excess. On street corners there were huge cauldrons filled with soups and greasy meat stews offered by sweaty cooks, who beat rhythmically on the tables with their serving implements. Alley after alley was filled with screaming and laughter and festival handkerchiefs waving over the dancers.

The king breathed the afternoon air with a growing relief from the weight that had pressed down heavily on his chest. The night came out of the foothills blurring the outlines of trees and labyrinths. Then Christophe saw that the musicians from the royal chapel were crossing the parade ground carrying their instruments. Each one came with his professional deformity. The harpist was bent over, hunched under the weight of his harp; that other one, the really skinny one, seemed pregnant with a drum hanging from his shoulders; another embraced a helicon. At the tail end of the group was a dwarf, almost hidden by a Chinese crescent that jingled at every step. The king was surprised that his musicians would enter the forest at that hour, as if they were going to give a concert at the foot of a solitary ceiba tree, when eight military kettledrums rolled simultaneously. It was the hour of the changing of the guard. His Majesty watched carefully over his grenadiers to make sure that, despite his illness, they still observed the strict discipline he had taught them. Suddenly the king's hand rose in a gesture of unexpected anger. The untuned drums were not playing the regimental rhythm but were falling into three different percussive movements, no longer produced by the sticks but by hands beating directly on the skins.

"They're playing the *mandoucouman*!" Christophe screamed, throwing his bicorn to the floor.

At that moment the guards broke ranks, crossing the parade ground haphazardly. The officers ran with drawn swords. Bunches of men dropped down out of the barracks windows with their coats open and pants over their boots.

Shots were fired into the air. A flag bearer tore apart the royal prince's crown-and-dolphin standard. Amid the confusion a platoon of light cavalry left the palace at a gallop, followed by mules pulling a van full of saddles and harnesses. It was a disordered mass of uniforms driven by military drums played with closed fists. Surprised by the mutiny, a soldier with malaria left the infirmary covered in a sheet, adjusting the strap of his shako. As he passed under Christophe's window he made an obscene gesture and escaped at a run. Later, during the calm of afternoon, all that was heard was the distant complaint of a peacock. The king turned his head. In the darkened room Queen Marie-Louise and the princesses Athénaïs and Améthyste were weeping. It became clear why there had been all that drinking among the people of Haut-le-Cap.

Christophe took to wandering around the palace, holding himself up with banisters, curtains, and the backs of chairs. The absence of courtiers, footmen, and guards lent a terrifying emptiness to the hallways and living rooms. The walls seemed taller, the floor tiles wider. The Hall of Mirrors reflected the lone figure of the king again and again into the hidden world of the farthest mirrors. And then that buzzing, that rubbing sound, that chirping of crickets he'd never heard before, came from the wood paneling in fits and starts, giving the silence depth and breadth. The candles melted slowly on the candelabra. A nocturnal butterfly flew about in the council chamber. Insects fell to the floor after flying into golden frames here

and there, making the incomparable sound of beetles crash-
ing against a hard surface. In the grand reception hall with
its windows open on two sides, Christophe heard the sound
of his own heels, which increased his sense of complete
solitude. Via a service door, he went down to the kitchen,
where the fire had died under meatless spits. On the floor,
next to the carving table, were several empty bottles of
wine. They had taken the strings of garlic that hung from
the chimney mantle, the strands of *djon-djon* mushrooms,
and the smoked hams. The palace was deserted, given over
to a moonless night. It belonged to whoever wanted to take
it, since even the hunting dogs were gone. Henri Christophe
returned to his floor. The white stairs were ominously cold
under the light of hanging chandeliers. A bat entered
through the skylight of the rotunda, flying around under
the burnished gold of the ceiling. The king leaned on the
balustrade, seeking the solidity of marble.

Down there, seated on the last step of the grand staircase, five young blacks had turned their anxious faces
toward him. At that moment, Christophe felt he loved them.
They were the Royal Bonbons: Deliverance, Valentin, La
Couronne, John, and Bien Aimé, the Africans the king had
bought from a slave trader and given their freedom so he
could teach them the fine trade of being pages. Christophe
had always kept himself apart from the African mysticism of the first rulers of Haitian independence, trying in
everything he did to give his court a European semblance.
But now that he found himself alone, after his dukes, bar-

ons, generals, and ministers had betrayed him, the only ones loyal to him were those five native Africans, born Congos, Fulas, or Mandingos, who sat and waited like faithful dogs, their butts planted on the cold marble of the stairs, an *Ultima Ratio Regum* that could no longer be imposed via the mouths of cannons. Christophe contemplated his pages a long time; he made a gesture of affection in their direction, to which they responded with a pathetic reverence, and he moved on to the throne room.

He stopped before the canopy adorned with his coat of arms. Two crowned lions held up a blazon imprinted with the emblem of the Crowned Phoenix and the device *I am born from my ashes*. A draped banner bore the motto *God, my cause and my sword*. Christophe opened a heavy chest hidden under a tasseled velvet cloth. He took out a handful of silver coins marked with his initials. Then he threw several solid gold crowns of different thicknesses on the floor. One of them reached the door and rolled down the staircase, making a noise that filled the whole palace. The king sat on his throne and watched the yellow candles of a candelabra melt down. Mechanically he recited the text that preceded all the public acts of his government: "I, Henri, by the Grace of God and the Constitutional Laws of the State, King of Haiti, Sovereign of the Islands of Tortue, Gonave, and other adjacent ones, Destroyer of Tyranny, Regenerator and Benefactor of the Haitian Nation, Creator of its Moral, Political, and Military Institutions, First Crowned Monarch of the New World, Defender of the Faith, Founder of the Royal and Military Order of Saint-Henri, salute all of you, now present and to come . . ." Christophe suddenly remembered the Citadelle of La Ferrière, his fortress built above the clouds.

But at that moment the night filled with drums. Calling one another, responding from mountain to mountain, rising from the beaches, coming out of the caves, running under the trees, descending down the ravines and through the riverbeds, the drums thundered, the Rada drums and the Congo drums and the drums of Bouckman, the drums of the Great Pact, all the drums of Vodou. It was a vast tumult of percussion advancing toward Sans-Souci, tightening in a circle, a horizon of thunder narrowing—a storm, the vortex of which was at that moment the throne without heralds or sergeants-at-arms. The king returned to his room and his window. The fire that engulfed his farms, his granges, and his sugarcane fields had already begun. Before the drums came the flames, jumping from house to house, from crop to crop. A flame flared in the granary, dropping scorched and burning boards into the hay barn. The north wind took the cinders from the cornfields and brought them ever closer. Burning ashes rained down on the palace terraces.

Henri Christophe thought again about the Citadelle. *Ultima Ratio Regum.* That fortress, the only one of its kind, was too large for a lone man, and the monarch had never thought that the day would come when he would find himself alone. The blood of the bulls the thick walls had drunk proffered protection only against the arms of the whites. But that blood had never been directed against the blacks, who, close as they were now ahead of the marching flames, invoked powers that demanded blood sacrifice. Christophe the reformer had wanted to ignore Vodou, creating a caste of Catholic gentlemen by force of the whip. Now he understood that the true traitors to his cause that night were Saint Peter with his key, the Capuchins of Saint Francis, the black Saint Benedict with the dark-faced Virgin in her blue cloak, the Evangelists, whose book he had made his subjects kiss in their oaths of loyalty, as well as all the martyrs, for whom he had ordered the lighting of candles containing thirteen golden coins. After glancing hatefully at the chapel's white cupola, filled with images that turned their backs on him and signs that had passed to the enemy, the king asked for clean clothes and perfumes. He made the princesses come out, and he dressed himself in his most sumptuous ceremonial vestments. He put on his broad two-colored sash, emblem of his investiture, tying it over the sword handle. The drums were so close that they seemed to be beating behind the iron fence of the parade ground, at the foot of a large staircase of stone. At that moment the palace mirrors caught on fire, both the glass and the frames, the crystal goblets, the crystal lamps, the glasses, the stained glass, and the nacre of the side tables. The fires were everywhere, the real ones mixing with their reflections. All the mirrors of Sans-Souci burned at once. The whole building had disappeared into that cold fire that emblazoned the night, making of each wall a pool of curling flames.

The shot was barely heard because the drums were so near. Christophe dropped the weapon and raised his hand to his wounded temple. His body lurched forward as if to take another step before falling headlong with all his decorations. The pages appeared in the threshold of the hall. The king lay dying, facedown in his own blood.

7

The Only Gate

The African pages left at a full run through a back door that led to the mountains. On their shoulders they carried in primitive fashion the trunk of a branch, trimmed by machete, from which hung a hammock. One of the monarch's spurs showed through the torn netting. Behind them in the darkness, constantly turning their heads and tripping on poinciana roots, were the princesses Athénaïs and Améthyste, wearing their servants' sandals, which made for easier footing, and the queen, who had thrown off her shoes when one of the heels broke on the stones of the path. Soliman, now a footman in the service of the king, brought up the rear with a rifle hanging from his shoulder and a machete in his hand. As they entered the canopied night of the heights, the fire below seemed denser, the flames closer together, even though it was slowing down around the edges of the parade ground. Nevertheless, on the side facing Milot the fire had reached the bales of hay inside the horse stables. From afar they could hear the whinnying that sounded like the wails of large children being tortured. The upper floor of the stable came down in a flurry of incandescent chips through which a maddened horse appeared with its mane singed and its tail burned to the bone. Suddenly many lights began to race through the building. It was a dance of torches that went from the kitchen to the attics, coming in through windows, going up balustrades, running along gutters, as if an incredible swarm of fireflies had taken control of the upper floors. The looting had begun. The pages quickened their pace, knowing that the spoils would delay the mutineers for a good while. Soliman cocked the rifle and placed the butt under his arm.

With dawn approaching the fugitives came to the outskirts of the Citadelle of La Ferrière. The trek became more difficult along the steep slope and over the many cannons that lay along the way without ever having reached their carriages and would rust away forever. The sea was becoming visible in the direction of Île de la Tortue when the chains of the drawbridge ran with a grating sound over the rocks. Slowly the studded doors of the Great Door opened. And the corpse of Henri Christophe entered boots first into his Escorial, wrapped in the hammock carried by the black pages. Heavier by the moment, it began to ascend the interior stairs, which were wet with the cold water dripping from the vaulted ceilings. Reveilles broke at dawn, answering one another from one end of the fortress to the other. Fully covered in red fungi, still in the thrall of darkness, the Citadelle emerged—bloody above, rust-colored below—out of the gray clouds that had be-come bloated from the smoke of the fires on the Plaine.

Once in the middle of the parade ground, the fugitives told their tragic story to the governor of the fortress. Soon the news had spread through the air vents, tunnels, and hallways to the bedrooms and living quarters. The soldiers began to appear everywhere, pushed forward by other soldiers coming down the stairs, deserting the batteries, descending from the watchtowers, and abandoning their posts. There was jubilant screaming in the patio of the main tower: prisoners released by their guards came out of their cells, moving with defiant joy in the direction of the royal family. Packed closer and closer together by the crowd, the pages with their headdresses undone, the barefoot queen, and the timid princesses defended by Soliman from insolent hands retreated slowly toward a mound of fresh mortar into which several shovels had been stuck and abandoned there by the bricklayers. Seeing that the situation was get-ting desperate, the governor gave the order to abandon the patio. A loud cackle rose over his voice. A prisoner, so di-sheveled that his sexual organ showed through his pants, raised a finger toward the queen's throat and said:

"In a country of whites, when the chief dies, his wife is decapitated."

Aware that the example given thirty years before by the idealists of the French Revolution was still fresh in the minds of his men, the governor thought everything was lost. But at that moment the rumor that the company of guards had gone down the mountain suddenly turned the tables. Men ran over one another through stairs and tunnels to get to the Great Door of the Citadelle. Jumping, sliding, and rolling they threw themselves down the mountain paths, looking for the fastest way to arrive at Sans-Souci. Henri Christophe's army had fallen apart and flowed downhill like a river. For the first time the enormous building was deserted, thereby gaining in the deep silence of its halls the funereal solemnity of a royal tomb.

The governor peeked into the hammock to study the semblance of His Majesty. He cut off one of Christophe's pinkies and gave it to the queen, who hid it in her neckline, feeling it slide toward her belly like a cold, slithering worm. Afterward, obeying an order, the pages placed the corpse over the mound of mortar, into which it began to sink slowly, faceup, as if pulled by viscous hands. The corpse had arched somewhat in the climb, as it was still warm when it was carried by the servants, and so his belly and thighs disappeared first, his arms and boots still floating uncertainly in the gloppy grayness of the mortar. Then only his face remained, held up by the shape of the bicorn that went from ear to ear. Fearing the mortar would harden without having covered the head fully, the governor placed his hand on the forehead of the king and pushed it down with a gesture akin to someone taking a sick man's temperature. At last the mix closed over the eyes of Henri Christophe, who continued on his slow descent into the entrails of a dampness that was becoming increasingly less malleable.

The corpse stopped descending, made one with the stone that imprisoned it. Having chosen his own death, Henri Christophe would never know the putrefaction of his flesh, the same flesh that became one with the very substance of the fortress, inscribed within its architecture and integrated into its body held up by buttresses. The whole mountain of the Bonnet à l'Évêque had become the mausoleum of Haiti's first king.

PART FOUR

I was afraid of those visions,
but once I saw these others,
my fear grew even deeper.

—Calderón

1

The Night of the Statues

As her bracelets and charms clinked on the keyboard of a newly bought pianoforte, Mademoiselle Athénaïs accompanied her sister, Améthyste, whose somewhat stringent voice enriched an aria from Rossini's *Tancredi* with languorous portamenti. Dressed in a white robe, with her forehead covered by a handkerchief tied in the Haitian style, Queen Marie-Louise was embroidering a tablecloth destined for the convent of the Capuchins of Pisa when she became annoyed by a cat that was batting around the balls of thread. Since those tragic days of the Dauphin Victor's execution and their escape from Port-au-Prince, facilitated by English merchants who had done business with the royal family, the princesses knew for the first time a European summer. Rome lived with open doors under a sun that shone on all the marble, bringing inside the stench of the monks and the calls of street vendors. The thousand bells of the city sounded lazily under a cloudless sky that reminded them of the skies of the Plaine in January. Sweaty and happy

that the heat had finally returned, Athénaïs and Améthyste
went about barefoot with their skirts unbuttoned; they
spent their days playing board games, making lemonade, and pulling off the shelf the latest novels, the covers
adorned with copper etchings in a new style, showing cemeteries at midnight, Scottish lakes, sylphs surrounding a
young hunter, and maidens leaving a love letter in the hole
of an old oak.

Soliman, too, was happy in that summery Rome. His
appearance on the narrow streets—damp with clothes drying on the line and dirty with cabbages, coffee grounds, and
other refuse—had provoked a scandalous uproar. Suddenly
the blindest *lazzaroni* opened their eyes and stopped playing their mandolins and barrel organs, the better to see the
black man. Other beggars shook their stumps furiously,
showing off their legacy of sores and other miseries in case
he was a foreign ambassador. The children followed him
everywhere, calling him King Balthasar and forming im-
promptu bands of kazoos and Jew's harps around him.
They gave him glasses of wine in the taverns. As he passed,
artisans came out of their stores, offering him a tomato or
a handful of nuts. It had been a long time since a black
man had shown his face in front of a façade by Flaminio
Ponzio or a portico by Antonio Labacco. He was asked to
tell his story, which Soliman embroidered with flowery fab-
rications, passing himself off as a nephew of Henri Christophe who had miraculously escaped the massacre of the
Cap the night that the firing squad had bayoneted one of

the monarch's illegitimate children after several discharges had failed to kill him. The simpletons listening to him did not have a very clear idea of the place where those events had occurred. Some thought about Madagascar or Persia or the country of the Berbers.

When he sweated, there was always someone who wanted to pat his cheeks with a handkerchief to see if the color came off. As a prank they took him one afternoon to one of the crowded and smelly theaters that put on comic operas. At the end of one about Italians in Algiers, he was pushed onto the stage. His unexpected entry raised such a ruckus in the orchestra seats that the company's manager asked him to do it again whenever he wanted. He was lucky enough to become the lover of a maid in the household of the Borghese Palace, a good-looking girl from the Piedmont who disliked wimpy men. On very hot days Soliman would take long siestas on the Forum lawns, where flocks of sheep were always grazing. The ruins gave pleasant shadows on the abundant grass, and when you dug the earth, it wasn't unusual to find a marble ear or a stone decoration or a moldy coin. Sometimes the place was chosen by a streetwalker to ply her trade with some errant seminarian or other. But it was visited mostly by studious people—clerics with green umbrellas, Englishmen with slender hands—who would wax poetic over a broken column, writing down the fragmented inscriptions. At dusk, the black man would enter the service stairs of the Borghese Palace with the Piedmontese woman and uncork several bottles of fine red wine. With the owners absent, the greatest disorder was the norm in the mansion. The lamps at the entrance were covered with flies, the liveries were all dirty, the coachmen always drunk, the carriage unpainted, and so many spiderwebs hung in the library that no one had dared enter it for years, so as not to feel the nasty little feet scurrying across their neck or inside their bra. Had a young abbot, a nephew of the prince, not been living in the upper floors, the servants would have taken over those rooms as well, sleeping in the beds where cardinals had once lain.

One late night when Soliman and the Piedmontese woman were by themselves in the kitchen, the black man, who was very drunk, wanted to go beyond the servants' bedrooms. Following a long corridor they came to an immense patio made of marble turned blue by the moon. Two rows of superimposed columns framed the patio, throwing the shadow of the capitals halfway up the wall. Pointing a street lantern up and down, the Piedmontese woman revealed to Soliman the world of statues that populated one of the side galleries. They were of naked women, almost all with veils blown by a slight breeze over the spots where decency might take them. There were many animals as well. Some of these ladies held a swan in their arms, embraced the neck of a bull, pranced among greyhounds, or fled from horned men with cloven hooves, who seemed somehow related to the devil. It was a white world, cold and motionless, the shadows of which moved and grew by the light of the lantern, as if all those creatures with shadowy eyes that looked without seeing gyrated around the midnight visitors. With the gift drunks have for seeing horrible things out of the corners of their eyes, Soliman was convinced he saw one of the statues lower her arm a bit. Somewhat bothered by that, he dragged the Piedmontese woman up a stairway that led to the upper rooms. Paintings appeared to jump out of the wall and come alive. Suddenly a smiling young man raised a curtain; he was an adolescent, crowned by grapevines, who held a flute to his mouth or raised his index finger to his lips calling for silence. After crossing a gallery lined with mirrors on which someone had painted flowers in oil, the maid made a mischievous gesture, opened a narrow walnut door, and lowered the lantern.

In the rear of that small room was a lone statue of a woman, lying naked on a bed, who seemed to be offering an apple. Soliman tried to shake his drunkenness away and approached the statue uncertainly. The surprise had sobered him up to some degree. That face and body, it all reminded him of someone. He touched the marble nervously, his sense of smell and sight in his hands. He felt the breasts. He moved one of his hands around them and over the belly and paused his little finger on the navel. He touched the gentle indentation of the spine, as if to turn the figure. His fingers searched for the roundness of the hips, the softness of the hamstrings, and the terseness of the chest. The voyage of his hands refreshed his memory, bringing images from far away. In previous times he'd been familiar with that shape. Using the same circular movement he had eased the pain of that ankle, immobilized by a sprain. The substance was different, but the forms were the same. He remembered now the nights of fear on Île de la Tortue when a French general lay dying behind a closed door. He remembered her, she who had to have her head scratched before going to bed. Suddenly, moved by a powerful physical memory, Soliman began to move his hands like a masseur, following the route of the muscles, the contour of the tendons, rubbing the back from the inside to the outside, feeling the pectorals with his thumbs, tapping here and there. Then the coldness of marble moving to his wrists like the pincers of death immobilized him in a scream. The wine turned on itself. That statue, tinted yellow by the light of the lamp, was the corpse of Pauline Bonaparte, recently hardened, recently stripped of heartbeat and sight, which could perhaps still be brought back to life. With a terrifying voice, as if his chest were being torn apart, the black man began to call out loudly inside the immensity of the Borghese Palace. And his figure became so primitive, his feet beat so hard on the floor, making a drum out of the chapel below, that the Piedmontese woman ran horrified down the stairs, leaving Soliman face-to-face with the Venus of Canova.

The patio filled with candles and lanterns. Awakened by the voice that resounded so loudly from the second floor, the footmen and coachmen came out of their rooms, wearing only their nightshirts and holding on to their underpants. The loud knock on the coaches' entrance sounded with an echo, opening the way for the gendarmes on evening rounds, who entered in single file, followed by several alarmed neighbors. Seeing the mirrors light up, the black man turned brusquely. The lights, the crowd of people gathered in the patio amid the white marble statues, the apparent silhouette of the bicorns, the uniforms decorated with light piping, and the cold curve of an unsheathed sword reminded him with a shiver of the night of Henri Christophe's death. Soliman threw a chair through a window and jumped to the street. And the early risers saw him, trembling with fever as a result of the malaria he had contracted from the Pontine Marshes, invoking Papa Legba to open the way back to Saint-Domingue. An intolerable nightmarish sensation covered his hands. It seemed he had fallen into a trance as a result of touching the stone of a grave, as happened to some of the possessed back home, who were both feared and revered by peasants because they were best able to communicate with the Lords of the Cemeteries.

It was hopeless for Queen Marie-Louise to try to calm him with a tea of bitter herbs, which she received directly from the Cap, through London, with the help of President Boyer. Soliman was cold. An unexpected fog dampened the marbles of Rome. The summer thickened hour by hour. Searching for a way of easing the servant's illness, the princesses sent for Doctor Antommarchi, who had been

Napoleon's doctor in Saint Helena and whose professional merits were well-known, especially as a homeopath. But the pills never left their box. With his back to everyone, whimpering at the wall decorated with yellow flowers on green paper, Soliman tried to reach a god to be found in distant Dahomey, in some shadowy road crossing, with his red phallus resting on a special crutch.

> *Papa Legba, l'ouvri barrié-a pou moin, agó yé,*
> *Papa Legba ouvri barrié-a pou moin, pou moin*
> *passé.*

2

The Royal House

Ti Noël was among those who initiated the looting of the
Palace of Sans-Souci, and quickly the remains of Lenormand de Mézy's old house were strangely furnished. The
ruins were still without a roof, since he could not find two
points of support on which to place a beam or a long pole,
but the old man had cleared some uneven stones with his
machete, uncovering parts of the foundation, a window
frame, three stairs, and a stretch of wall that still showed
some of the molding of the old Norman dining room. The
night in which the Plaine had filled with men, women,
and children carrying pendulum clocks, chairs, canopies,
candelabra, prayer stools, lamps, and washbasins, Ti Noël
had gone back and forth to Sans-Souci several times. As a
result he had a *boule* table standing in front of the chimney with the hay floor that served as his bedroom, which
he hid from sight with a Chinese folding screen, painted
with dim figures on a background of faded gold. A stuffed
moonfish, a gift from the Royal Society of London to Prince

Victor, lay on the last broken floor tiles through which roots and wild grasses grew next to a small music box and a thick glass bottle filled with multicolored bubbles. He had also taken a doll dressed as a shepherdess, an upholstered armchair, and three volumes of the *Grande Encyclopédie*, on which he would sit to chew on sugarcane.

But what made the old man happiest was a dress coat that had once belonged to Henri Christophe himself, made of green silk with salmon-colored lace cuffs, that he wore at all times with a straw hat flattened and shaped like a bicorn on which he stuck a red flower as decoration. In the afternoons he could be seen surrounded by the furniture he had arranged in the open, playing with the doll that opened and closed its eyes or winding the music box that repeated the same German Ländler from dawn to dusk. Now Ti Noël spoke constantly. He spoke with his arms spread open in the middle of the road; he spoke to the washerwomen kneeling by the sandy streams with naked breasts; he spoke to the children dancing in a circle. But he spoke, above all, when he sat at his table and held a guava branch as a scepter. To his mind came vague memories of things told by one-armed Mackandal so many years ago that he couldn't say when exactly. In those days he began to be certain that he had a mission to accomplish, even though no sign or revelation came to him as to the exact nature of the mission. But it was something big, something worthy of someone who has lived so many years on the earth and has left behind an unknown number of children, who concerned themselves only with their own children, on both sides of the sea. Besides, it was clear that great moments were about to be lived. When the women saw him coming down a path, they waved white handkerchiefs as a sign of reverence, like the Sunday palms that had once honored Jesus. When he walked by a hut, the old women invited him to sit, bringing him a bit of white rum in a gourd or a newly rolled cigar. At a drum ceremony, Ti Noël became possessed by the king of Angola and gave a long speech filled with riddles and promises. Later, flocks of sheep appeared on his lands. Those new creatures grazing among the ruins were, no doubt, gifts from his subjects. Seated on his chair with his coat open and his straw hat tight around his head, he scratched his naked belly slowly and gave orders to the wind. But they were the edicts of a peaceful kingdom, since no tyranny of whites or blacks seemed to threaten his freedom. The old man filled with beautiful things the spaces between the remains of the walls and made any passerby a minister, anyone clearing land a general. He gave away baronies, offered garlands, and blessed young girls, paying services rendered with flowers. In this manner he founded the Order of the Bitter Broom, the Order of the Christmas Bonus, the Order of the Hibiscus Flower, and the Order of the Night Jasmine. But the most coveted of all was the Order of the Sunflower because it was the most beautiful. Since the half-tiled floor that functioned as the Hall of Audience was very good for dancing, his palace would fill with peasants who brought bamboo pipes, *chá-chás*, and kettledrums. Lighted poles were placed in the crooks of the branches, and Ti Noël, smug as ever in his green dress coat, presided over the party, seated between a Father of the Savannah, representing a church founded long ago by runaway slaves, and an old veteran, who had fought against Rochambeau in Vertières and who still kept his battle uniform for solemn occasions. Its blues were faded and its reds had turned strawberry from all the rain that leaked into his house.

3

The Surveyors

One morning the Surveyors appeared. One had to have seen them moving about to understand the horror inspired by the presence of those insect-like beings. The Surveyors came from faraway Port-au-Prince, over the cloud-covered mountains, and descended into the Plaine. They were quiet men, very light-skinned, dressed—it's important to recognize—in a rather normal fashion, who unrolled long ribbons on the ground, drove stakes down, carried plumbs, looked through tubes, and bristled with rulers and set squares. When Ti Noël saw that those suspicious characters came and went through his domain, he spoke to them seriously. The Surveyors, however, paid no attention to him. They went from here to there insolently, measuring everything and noting things down in gray notebooks with thick carpenter pencils. The old man noticed angrily that they spoke in the language of the French, a language he had forgotten since the time when Monsieur Lenormand de Mézy had wagered him at a card game in

Santiago de Cuba. Ti Noël ordered the sons-of-bitches to get away, screaming in such a fashion that one of the Surveyors grabbed him by the nape, pushing him out of the field of vision of his lens with a ruler blow to the belly. The old man hid in his chimney, sticking his head out from behind the Chinese screen to bark insults. The next day, wandering about the Plaine in search of something to eat, he noticed that the Surveyors were everywhere and that some mulattoes on horseback, with their open shirt collars, silk sashes around the waist, and military boots were directing huge tillage and demarcation operations by hundreds of blacks under guard. Riding their donkeys, carrying chickens and pigs, many peasants abandoned their huts amid the screaming and weeping of their women to seek refuge in the mountains. Ti Noël learned from a fugitive that agricultural labor had become obligatory and that the whip was now in the hands of Republican mulattoes, the new masters of the Plaine du Nord.

Mackandal had never foreseen the matter of forced labor. Neither had Bouckman the Jamaican. The mulattoes in control was a novelty that could never have been imagined by José Antonio Aponte, the Cuban black rebel leader decapitated by the Marquis of Someruelos, whose story Ti Noël learned about during his days as a Cuban slave. Certainly, not even Henri Christophe could have guessed that the lands of Saint-Domingue were to foster an aristocracy between two waters, this quadroon caste that was now taking over the old plantations, the privileges, and the investitures. The old man raised his clouded eyes toward the Citadelle of La Ferrière. But his vision could no longer reach that far. The word of Henri Christophe had become stone and was not among us. Of his powerful body all that remained, there in Rome, was a finger floating in a vial of rock crystal filled with alcohol. And to continue that practice, Queen Marie Louise, after taking her daughters to the baths at Carlsbad, had stated in her will that her right foot should be preserved in alcohol by the Capuchins of Pisa in a chapel built thanks to her own munificence. No matter how hard he thought, Ti Noël couldn't find a way of helping his subjects, newly bent under somebody's lash. The old man was beginning to get desperate seeing this unending return of chains, this rebirth of shackles, this proliferation of miseries, which the least hopeful accepted as proof of the uselessness of any sort of revolt. Ti Noël feared as well that they would make him work in the fields, despite his age, and thoughts of Mackandal came once again to his memory. Since the vestment of man brought so many calamities, it was best to leave it for a time, following the events in the Plaine in less obvious guise. Once he made this decision, Ti Noël was surprised at how easy it was to transform oneself into an animal when one had the necessary powers. As proof he climbed a tree, wanting to be a bird, and immediately became a bird. He looked to the Surveyors from atop a branch, sticking his beak into the pulp of a star apple. The next day he wanted to be a stallion and he became a stallion, but he had to run away from a mulatto who tried to lasso him in order to castrate him with a kitchen knife. As a wasp he soon tired of the monotonous geometries of wax architecture. Transforming himself into an ant was a bad idea. He was forced to carry enormous loads through endless paths, under the vigilance of big-headed soldiers who reminded him all too closely of Lenormand de Mézy's overseers, Christophe's guards, and the mulattoes of today. At times, the hooves of a horse destroyed a column of workers, killing hundreds before the big-headed soldiers would once again bring order to the file, the path was once again determined, and everything was as before, the same busy coming and going. Ti Noël was merely in disguise; nevertheless, he felt a certain solidarity with the species, and he took refuge by himself under his table, which was, that night, his protection against a steady drizzle that raised over the fields the haylike odor of wet grass.

4

Agnus Dei

It was going to be a hot day with low clouds. The spider-webs were just drying from the night rains when a great commotion came down from heaven over the lands of Ti Noël. Running and tripping as they landed, the geese from the old pens of Sans-Souci—spared from the looting because blacks didn't like their flesh—had lived freely all this time in mountain ravines. Happy at their visit, the old man took them in with a great fuss, since he was well acquainted with the intelligence and joy of the goose, having observed the exemplary life those birds led when Monsieur Lenormand de Mézy long ago tried unsuccessfully to acclimatize them. Since they were not creatures made for heat, the females laid only five eggs every two years. But their attitude inspired a series of rituals that were passed on from generation to generation. On a bank of shallow water the nuptials took place in front of the whole clan of geese and ganders. A young male mated with a female for life, covering her in the midst of a chorus of joyful honking accompanied by a liturgical dance composed of gyrations, kicks, and turns of the neck. Then the whole clan partici- pated in building the nest. During incubation the wife was protected by all the males, alert all night, even if they did stick their heads under their wings. When danger threat- ened the clumsy chicks dressed in yellow down, the oldest gander charged with his beak and chest the intruding mastiff, rider, or wagon. The geese were an ordered folk, fundamentally and systematically so, whose existence did not tolerate having one individual stand above others of the same species. The principle of their authority, embodied by the Arch-Gander, was to use the minimum to maintain order within the clan, as would a king or the overseer of one of the old African councils. Tired of risky transforma- tions, Ti Noël used his extraordinary powers to change himself into a goose and thus live among the birds that had taken residence in his domain.

But when he tried to join the clan, he was warned by sharp beaks and strong necks to keep his distance. He was forced into a corner of a pasture by a wall of white feathers surrounding the indifferent females. Then Ti Noël tried to be discreet by not imposing himself and approving what the others had to say. He found only disdain and shrugging wings. It was of no use that he revealed to the females the place to find the most delicious watercress. The gray tails moved with disgust, and the yellow eyes looked at him with arrogant mistrust. The clan now seemed like an aristo- cratic community, completely closed to any individual of a different caste. The Arch-Gander of Sans-Souci would have rejected any contact with the Arch-Gander of Dondón. Had they encountered each other face-to-face, a war would have started. For this reason Ti Noël soon understood that no matter if he tried for years, he would never have the least access to the rites and roles of the clan. He was led to comprehend fully that it was not enough to be a goose in order to believe that all geese were equal. No known goose had sung or danced on his wedding day. None alive had witnessed his birth. He presented himself without the least proof of the purity of his blood before geese who could trace their ancestry back several generations. In short, he was an outlander.

Ti Noël understood darkly that the rejection by the geese was punishment for his cowardice. Mackandal had disguised himself as an animal for years to serve humans, not to abandon their territory. At that moment, once again as a human being, the old man had a supreme moment of understanding. In a heartbeat he lived through the key moments of his life: he saw once again the heroes who had revealed to him the strength and abundance of his ancestors in Africa, allowing him to believe in all the possible manifestations of the future. He felt he was hundreds of years old. A cosmic exhaustion, as of a planet weighed down with stones, fell on his shoulders, stooped from so many beatings, sweats, and rebellions. Ti Noël had spent his inheritance, and in spite of having reached his ultimate poverty, he was leaving behind the same inheritance he had received. He was a body of wasted flesh. And he understood now that man never knows for whom he suffers and waits. He suffers and waits and works for people he'll never know, and who likewise will suffer and wait and work for others who won't be happy either, since man always longs for a happiness that lies just beyond that which is given to him. But the greatness of man lies precisely in wanting to improve on what already is by taking on labors. There is no greatness to achieve in the Kingdom of Heaven, since it has an already established order, the unknown made clear, existence without end, without the possibility of sacrifice, rest, and delight. That's why, burdened by sorrows and labors, beautiful within his misery, capable of loving in the midst of plagues, man can find his greatness, his greatest measure, only in the Kingdom of This World.

Ti Noël got up on his table, scuffing the marquetry with his calloused feet, and looked in the direction of the city of the Cap. The sky had turned black with the smoke of fires, like the night in which all the conch shells of the mountain and the coast had sung. The old man launched his declaration of war against the new owners, ordering his subjects to leave immediately and assault the insolent works of the new invested mulattoes. At that moment, a great green wind coming from the ocean fell over the Plaine du Nord, rushing through the valley of Dondón with a huge roar. And while the sacrificed bulls wailed in the heights of the

Bonnet à l'Évêque, the armchair, the screen, the encyclo-
pedia volumes, the music box, the doll, and the moonfish
suddenly took flight in the destruction of the last ruins of
the old plantation. All the trees lay down, their tops lean-
ing to the south, their roots pulled out of the ground.
Through the night, the sea turned rain left its salt on the
mountainsides.

From then on, no one knew anything about Ti Noël
or his green coat with salmon-colored cuffs, except, perhaps,
the wet vulture, seeker of all death, who waited for the sun
with outspread wings: a cross of feathers, which finally
folded and flew down into the thick foliage of the Bois
Cayman.

Afterword

by Pablo Medina

What has kept readers coming back to *The Kingdom of This World* over the years, what makes it a particularly resonant book in today's world, is not its stature as a literary masterpiece or the intricate play of its structure, but the significance of the themes it embodies. Foremost among these are race and class. Like Mark Twain before him, Carpentier tackles slavery head-on and in so doing helps us to understand the awful legacy of racial discrimination with which our society still struggles. These days, when we regularly see the results of racism and classism played out on television screens around the globe, the relevance of *The Kingdom of This World* cannot be overstated. This is a book about the clash of cultures and races; it is a book about overwhelming social injustice; it is, above all, a book about the good and the evil that people will inflict on one another. We may seek solace in the way the forces of nature blow everything to the ground and Death swoops down over rich and poor, black and white, in equal measure. In the final analysis, however, *The Kingdom of This World* is not a comforting book but a compellingly honest one.

Alejo Carpentier (1904–1980) was born to a French father and a Russian mother in Lausanne, Switzerland. Soon after his birth, his family emigrated to Cuba, and Alejo was raised in Havana, which he eventually claimed as his birth city. Both his parents were musicians and the young Alejo inherited their musical talents. He wrote opera librettos and ballets, but his musical abilities were superseded by his interest in literature. By the age of twenty he had devoted himself principally to writing fiction, although he never abandoned his interest in music, writing articles and essays on Cuban music that culminated in *Music in Cuba* (1946), an influential history that emphasized Cuban music's African roots alongside its European foundations. Carpentier traveled widely and lived for extended periods in Paris (1928–1939), where he was exposed to the avant-garde movements flourishing in that city, as well as in Venezuela (1945–1959), where he absorbed many of the intellectual and cultural currents of Latin America. He returned to Cuba after the triumph of the revolution and died in Paris in 1980.

Carpentier wrote a number of seminal works of fiction that engaged the culture and history of the Caribbean, but it was in *The Kingdom of This World*, written after the author's extended stay in Haiti in 1943, that he fully confronted the question of slavery and its impact on the social, cultural, spiritual, and political fabric of the Americas.

Novels, we know, are as much about people as they are about places, and Carpentier was most impressed by the Haitian people, their resilience and optimism in the face of obstacles history put in their way. Inspired in part by the ideals of the French Revolution, the Haitians gained independence from France in 1804 after their own revolutionary struggles and created a country where slavery was banned forever and human beings were free to pursue their individual and collective destinies. With few other models to draw from, the early Haitian leaders tried but failed to reproduce European governing systems. Among these leaders was Henri Christophe, who built the palace of Sans-Souci and the Citadelle of La Ferrière, which figure prominently in *The Kingdom of This World*. Christophe declared himself king and tried to imitate in dress and manners the French royal court while ignoring the African customs and beliefs that the Haitian people inherited from their forebears.

The Kingdom of This World is a novel in which history, destiny, and nature shape the thoughts and actions of its characters. Carpentier's book implies that only through a spirit forged and fortified by faith and ritual can human beings survive the forces threatening to destroy them. The spirit trumps the psyche at every turn. The characters defy psychological interpretation. The slave Ti Noël and his master, Monsieur Lenormand de Mézy, the two most fully drawn figures in the book, have both been stripped of their dignity and humanity by slavery. They are individuals, but they stand primarily as reflections of the universal impulses that drive and control humans in time. There are no heroes in *The Kingdom of This World*. Monsieur Lenormand de Mézy, his spirit corrupted by his participation in the slave trade, is, at times, more beast than human. Whenever he can get away with it, Ti Noël rapes and kills with the same impunity as his master. Good and evil revolve around each other while neither gains the upper hand.

Carpentier saw in Haiti a microcosm of much of the American continent outside the United States. European customs and culture could hardly be adapted to American reality. He was particularly adamant that American art and literature abandon European styles, such as surrealism and expressionism, and develop a new way of seeing (*lo real maravilloso*) that could explore more immediately the shaping of the human spirit in the American environment.

Carpentier had a notable influence on later generations of writers who would eventually form part of the Hispanic American canon. Gabriel García Márquez is said to have rewritten parts of *One Hundred Years of Solitude* after reading *The Kingdom of This World*. Carlos Fuentes and Mario Vargas Llosa, among others, show clear evidence of Carpentier's vision, as do younger writers such as Isabel Allende, Reinaldo Arenas, and Roberto Bolaño. Carpentier remains one of the most influential Hispanic American writers and *The Kingdom of This World* one of his most enduring works.